Alarming Awakening

Emaline knew quite well she had to be on her guard. Not only was she traveling alone in a closed coach with a man—but that man was Lord Liam Whitcomb, who had made no secret of his doubts about her virtue

Despite the danger, however, she had yielded to her need for sleep. And when she woke, she discovered what folly there had been.

She was nestled in Lord Liam's strong arms, her soft body against his superbly muscular frame. Her flame-colored hair teased his lips, and it was clear he wanted nothing more than to press those lips on hers.

But that was not the worst of it. For she suddenly realized that her own arms had gone under his jacket and around his waist. Not only that, but she was on his side of the coach, pressing him against the door.

If she had done that in her sleep, what was she capable of awake? And for the first time in her innocent life, Emaline suspected it was not only male lust she had to guard against, but her own no longer dormant desire. . . .

SIGNET REGENCY ROMANCE
Coming in May 1996

Evelyn Richardson
The Reluctant Heiress

Patricia Oliver
The Colonel's Lady

Emma Lange
The Irish Rake

Barbara Allister
The Frustrated Bridegroom

1-800-253-6476
ORDER DIRECTLY
WITH VISA OR MASTERCARD

The Ruby Necklace

by

Martha Kirkland

A SIGNET BOOK

SIGNET
Published by the Penguin Group
Penguin Books USA Inc., 375 Hudson Street,
New York, New York 10014, U.S.A.
Penguin Books Ltd, 27 Wrights Lane,
London W8 5TZ, England
Penguin Books Australia Ltd, Ringwood,
Victoria, Australia
Penguin Books Canada Ltd, 10 Alcorn Avenue,
Toronto, Ontario, Canada M4V 3B2
Penguin Books (N.Z.) Ltd, 182–190 Wairau Road,
Auckland 10, New Zealand

Penguin Books Ltd, Registered Offices:
Harmondsworth, Middlesex, England

First published by Signet, an imprint of Dutton Signet,
a division of Penguin Books USA Inc.

First Printing, April, 1996
10 9 8 7 6 5 4 3 2 1

Copyright © Martha Kirkland, 1996
All rights reserved

 REGISTERED TRADEMARK—MARCA REGISTRADA

Printed in the United States of America

Without limiting the rights under copyright reserved above, no part of this
publication may be reproduced, stored in or introduced into a retrieval system, or
transmitted, in any form, or by any means (electronic, mechanical, photocopying,
recording, or otherwise), without the prior written permission of both the copyright
owner and the above publisher of this book.

BOOKS ARE AVAILABLE AT QUANTITY DISCOUNTS WHEN USED TO PROMOTE PRODUCTS OR
SERVICES. FOR INFORMATION PLEASE WRITE TO PREMIUM MARKETING DIVISION, PENGUIN BOOKS
USA INC., 375 HUDSON STREET, NEW YORK, NEW YORK 10014.

If you purchased this book without a cover you should be aware that this book is
stolen property. It was reported as "unsold and destroyed" to the publisher and
neither the author nor the publisher has received any payment for this "stripped
book."

A special thank-you to Joyce Flaherty for her help,
to Carol Otten (AKA Tena Carlisle) for her support,
and to Daniel J. Norwood for his good taste

Chapter 1

"Damnation!" said Major Joel William Whitcomb, late of His Majesty's Hussars. "Will this feud never be finished?"

"It would appear not, sir," replied the solicitor. "I trust I acted properly in apprising you of Lord Seymour's intentions."

The major paused in his swift pacing of the snug, book-lined library, gazing out onto a charming prospect of lawn and beyond that to the expansive parkland. In his fury, he seemed to notice none of the beauty, nor did he note the thick shrubs and trees still lush and green, even though August was drawing to a close. "*You* acted properly, Mr. Mason. I cannot say the same for my father's cousin. Have you any thoughts on how we can put a stop to this latest scheme?"

"Regrettably, sir, I have nothing of merit to suggest."

Percival Mason shifted uneasily in the red leather wing chair, crossing one long, bony leg over the other. He wished he had a suitable suggestion, as much to prove his worth to his new employer as to see a smile return to Liam's angry face. Since returning from the war, the lad seemed to have forgotten how to smile.

The solicitor had been employed as Mr. Edgar Whitcomb's man of business for most of Liam's thirty-one years, and during that time he had watched a teasing, mischievous schoolboy grow to be a fun-loving, well-liked youth. In time the youth had developed into a daring yet personable young man—sought after by the ladies and a favorite with his regimental comrades. Mr. Mason studied the man who stood at the window. It was as if the Liam of his memories no longer existed, replaced by a quiet gentleman who seemed to feel the weight of the world upon his shoulders.

And yet, who could wonder at the change?

So much had happened to Liam Whitcomb in the past sixteen months. He had returned from the battle of Toulouse, gravely wounded, only to find that Mr. Edgar Whitcomb had been felled by a heart attack. And now, after taking his place as his father's successor, he found himself the target of his kinsman's latest attack.

"I am at a loss as to what should be done, Major."

"Of course you are, for who would believe that such enmity could be passed from one generation to the next?"

"I cannot be certain of this, Major, but I believe Lord Seymour's vindictiveness has less to do with your great-grandfather preferring his youngest grandson, and more to do with your father having gone to India and earning a fortune. Though why his lordship should be so resentful of his cousin, I do not know. Especially after Mr. Edgar expended large sums of money, on more than one occasion, to buy Lord Seymour out of his most pressing debts.

"I had assumed," he continued, "that your father's death would put an end to his lordship's hatred. Apparently I erred in that assumption. I never dreamed that lacking his cousin as an object for his enmity, Lord Seymour would see fit to visit his bitterness upon the next generation. But if such a thought had occurred to me, I still would not know what to advise under the present circumstances. How does one stop a man who is in possession of his mental faculties from seeking a new wife? Even such a wife as he proposes?"

The major clasped his long-fingered hands behind his back, as if to restrain them, making the solicitor wonder if he harbored thoughts of stopping his cousin by brute force. He was certainly capable of doing so. Though still somewhat slender after the extended period of recuperation needed as a result of the wounds sustained in battle, Liam Whitcomb was, nonetheless, a fine figure of a man, tall above average and possessing the toned muscles of a natural athlete.

A young Norse god, the ladies had used to call him, with his dark blond hair and his blue eyes. Unfailingly charming and seemingly indestructable in his athletic prowess and good health, he had been a favorite with the younger females. For the older ladies, it was his sunny disposition and his father's wealth that made him a *premier parti*.

Though his ready smile and his lively sense of humor were no longer in evidence, his physical strength had returned. And with the return to health had come a deep-seated instinct to protect those he loved. The solicitor shivered for the unsuspecting Lord Seymour's sake.

Nothing more was said until the younger man turned from the window, walked over to a massive satinwood kneehole desk, and perched on the edge, sitting forward, one hand resting on his muscular thigh. Except for the thin scar that began just below the major's left ear and trailed a full two inches along the edge of his strong jaw—a near-fatal saber wound inflicted by one of Napoleon's officers—his handsome face appeared calm, almost peaceful. Mr.

Mason might have been betrayed into thinking his employer's earlier anger gone, had he not seen the fire that burned in the dark blue eyes.

The younger man's stare pinned him to his chair. Stars in heaven! He could almost feel sorry for Lord Seymour. With such a look, the major must have turned young subalterns into quivering blancmange.

"If our cousin had aimed his vitriol at me, I could have shrugged it off. Unfortunately, he made my sister the target for this latest outrage, and for that reason I cannot let it pass. A man who would seek to hurt an innocent girl, a miss only just turned eighteen, must be made to see the error of his ways."

Possibly unaware he did so, Liam opened his bottle-green coat, his right hand moving to his side, as if seeking the hilt of a sword, a sword that no longer hung there. "This will be my cousin's final attack upon my family. This time he will listen to reason, or he will pay the price."

The solicitor swallowed a sudden obstruction in his throat, happy not to be his lordship, for Liam Whitcomb was not a man to make idle threats. Though he doubted that threats were often needed. A soldier for ten years, the major was a man accustomed to giving orders—life-and-death orders—and equally accustomed to having them obeyed.

"Did your informant discover my cousin Ambrose's whereabouts? Might I find him at his town house?"

"At the moment he is situated at Seymour Park. His agent was to procure the license at Doctor's Commons, see to the selection of a Covent Garden impure—preferably one with flaming hair—then convey both license and female to Wiltshire as soon as possible. His lordship planned to keep secret the existence of his prostitute wife, then surprise you by parading her before the *ton* on the night of Miss Cordia's introduction to society."

"He will not do so."

The softly spoken words caused Mr. Mason to squirm in his chair. "I hope you may be right, Major, for I need not tell you what such an association would do to Miss Cordia's chances of forming an eligible connection. They would be destroyed. Utterly destroyed. Even her very handsome portion of fifteen thousand would not be sufficient inducement to any respectable family should the head of your family align himself with a female of ill repute."

Liam pushed away from the desk and strode across the room to the bellpull, whose silent summons was answered in a matter of seconds. "Yes, sir?" enquired the young footman, bowing respectfully.

"Inform Harvey that I will need the carriage within the hour. Tell him our destination is Wiltshire. He will know what needs to be done."

Still awed by the new master of Whitcomb Hall, the footman bowed low. "Yes, sir. I will inform Mr. Harvey immediately."

Satisfied that his wishes would be carried out, Liam beckoned his man of business to join him at the far end of the room, where a trestled writing table stood upon a thick Turkey carpet. The dark oak surface of the table was very nearly obscured by dozens of large sheets of paper, some of which bore architectural drawings, while others listed building-construction specifications.

"And now," Liam said, "to the purpose for which I summoned you. I wish you to show these rough plans to an architect, one who is both competent and willing to start work immediately. He will, of course, make any necessary changes to the drawings, keeping in mind that function and accessibility are my primary objectives."

Surprised at this turn of events, Mr. Mason looked at the well-executed sketches. "Have you in mind to make an addition to Whitcomb Hall?"

"No," Liam answered, not unkindly, "the hall suits me as it is. I will leave its embellishment to future generations."

"Future generations?" The solicitor's thin face was alight with interest. "Am I to wish you happy, then, Major? You must know it was your father's most cherished dream that once you left the army, you would choose a suitable young lady to wed and start your nursery."

"Yes," Liam said, "I know my father longed to see the house filled to overflowing with little Whitcombs, and perhaps my sister will fulfill that dream. As for me, however, pursuing suitable young ladies must wait for a more convenient time. For now, I am much more interested in these plans."

Firmly, albeit politely, recalled to business, the solicitor gave his attention to the drawings upon the table.

"These plans," Liam began, "are for a Benevolent Institution—one I hope will answer the needs of at least a few of those soldiers who will be returning from the Continent soon, wounded and requiring a clean, healthful place in which to recuperate."

The solicitor could not stop his glance from sliding to his employer's left leg, where he knew the major had caught a French bullet. The recuperation from that wound had needed several months. The healing had obviously been a complete success, however, for Liam walked with grace and assurance, and without the least trace of a limp.

Noting the solicitor's glance, Liam said, "Bullets make no distinction between officers and the rank and file. They tear the flesh of either with equal ferocity. Unfortunately, the healing process is not so democratic. Not every soldier is as fortunate as I, to return to a home where a solicitous staff and a gentle sister provide needed care. Many have no one to sustain them while their minds and bodies mend. I cannot give them families, but I can at least supply a clean bed and good, hot food. And the sooner we begin the construction of the building, the sooner those beds can be put to use."

While Liam and Mr. Mason stood before the writing table, studying the plans for the Benevolent Institution, a hundred miles away, in the village of Bartholsby, Wiltshire, two women stood before an old traveling trunk, folding and packing the earthly possessions of the late Reverend Josiah Harrison.

"The rectory won't never be the same," Pegeen O'Shea said, sniffing loudly. "Not with your sainted father—God rest his soul—gone this twelvemonth, and you about to leave us. Sure and I'll never love working for the new family, not the way I loved doing for you and your dear papa."

Miss Emaline Agnes Harrison laid her hand upon the plump shoulder of the middle-aged woman who had been both servant and friend to her for most of her twenty-seven years. "Hush, do, Pegeen. If you go all Irish on me, we shall both fall into a fit of the dismals. Then I shall never be ready when young Georgie comes with his dogcart to take me to Lyle. The mail coach for London leaves in seven hours, and that is little enough time when there is still so much to sort through."

"It's Irish I am, Miss Emaline, and have been these fifty years, as well you know, so I'll no be apologizing for being sentimental. And if you think to bamboozle me into believing you are as unmoved as you appear, then you can just think again. Sure and I've known you too long to be taken in by that calm face and all your chattering about kicking up a rare lark in London. Your heart must be fair breaking, and that's a fact, for 'tis leaving the only home you've ever known, you are. As well to cry now and be done with it, I say!"

Resisting the tempting invitation to let down her defenses and give in to the sadness that gripped her heart, Emaline removed the last of the reverend's shirts from the clothespress and held the linen to her face for a moment, breathing in the lingering smell of her father that clung to the soft material. With trembling fingers she folded the garments neatly and placed them in the trunk.

After closing the lid and fastening the heavy metal clasps, she hid her betraying hands in the pockets of the large apron that protected her dress. "That is the last of it," she said quietly. "After I leave for Lyle, please have someone take the trunk over to the workhouse. Papa would want the poor to have his things."

Her knees suddenly unsteady, Emaline crossed to the bedroom window to sit on the little black lacquered settee where she had sat as a child, watching her mother at her dressing table, brushing her long, dark hair. Times out of mind the young girl had sat entranced, studying her mother's delicate hands as they braided the thick tresses, then wound the braid into a figure-eight at the back of her head.

Emaline had adopted her mother's hairstyle—the length of her hair all she shared in common with the gentle Jane Harrison. In all other ways she was her father's child. From her determined chin to her brown eyes and her coppery red hair, she was a feminine version of Josiah Harrison.

"What's to be done with your ma's workbox?" Pegeen asked, bringing Emaline's attention back to the present and the unpleasant task of packing her few personal possessions and those of her parents. The following day would see the arrival of the new spiritual leader of Bartholsby, and Emaline wanted to be gone before that time. She had no wish to witness another family take possession of the rectory.

Studying the pretty rosewood workbox with its blue velvet bag—a wedding gift to her mother from her grandfather, Sir Gerald Conklin—Emaline blinked back the moisture that threatened to spill from her eyes. Not wanting Pegeen to see her tears, she turned to stare fixedly at the honey-colored stone of St. Andrew's Church across the lane.

"I have no place for the box, Pegeen. I no longer have a home."

"You could have one within the hour if you'd but purchase that little cottage by the brook. With the sixty pounds per annum from your grandfather's trust, we could live in fine twig. I could keep house for you, as I've done this past year, and—"

"No, Pegeen. Not today, at any rate."

"When's it to be, then?"

"I cannot say. Certainly not before I have grown weary of exploring new places. I mean to enjoy my time as a rootless vagabond, and though I shall miss you, and my home and Bartholsby, I have a hunger to experience something other than this little village. Plays, museums, wondrous buildings—I have a thirst to see everything. And only after I have drunk my fill will I return to Wiltshire and that little cottage. Until then, dear friend, will you keep the workbox for me?"

"Faith, and you know I will."

Lifting the corner of her large apron, Pegeen wiped the moisture from her own eyes. "And don't you be thinking I'm so old I've forgotten what it's like to be young and wanting a little merriment. It's deserving it, you are. After this last year, caring for your father with such tenderness, and with never a complaint, 'tis little enough reward to treat yourself to a view of the city and a few innocent pleasures."

"I have had my reward already—as happy a childhood as any girl could want—with a father and mother who loved each other and still found plenty of love to spare for me."

"You deserve more, I'm thinking. So good as you were to himself, not to mention the way you stepped in and took over the work of the parish after Miss Jane died. Sure and no rector's wife could have done a better job, nor shown more concern for the sick and the poor."

"Please hush," Emaline said, her voice not quite steady. "I truly do not wish to continue this discussion."

"I'll hush right enough, dearie. But if it's wishes we're talking about, *I* wish you were packing to go on a wedding trip with a fine husband. I mislike the idea of you being at the beck and call of some crotchety old she-dragon."

Emaline turned to face her old friend. "I am persuaded you would like it even less if I were planning to live in London alone."

"The Blessed Mary and Joseph!" Pegeen gasped, crossing herself. "Tell me you'd never think of doing such a thing."

"No. I would not, for I am not that foolish. And since I cannot afford to hire a companion of my own, the next-best course is to hire myself out as one. Mrs. Zuber is a respectable lady, one who makes frequent visits to her daughters' homes in the country, not to mention a fortnight's stay at Tunbridge Wells each summer, so I shall be racketing about quite often, seeing a bit of the world. As for her being a she-dragon, I am persuaded I shall meet with kindness from her."

"Humph! If it's *kindness* you're after, you should have accepted Mr. Goodman when you had the chance. He would have treated you kind enough, did you but let him. Fair taken with you, he was. Always calling you his alabaster goddess, and such blarney."

"When it came to the sticking point, I found I could not commit to spending the rest of my life with Frank."

"Humph," the older woman said again. "Fair shocked I was, to hear you'd whistled him down the wind. When a lass reaches seven and twenty, she soon finds that upstanding men like Mr. Goodman don't come along every day."

How could Emaline explain to the older woman that Frank Goodman—worthy man that he was—was dull. With his practiced speeches and his gauche attempts at gallantry, he had never ignited so much as a spark inside her. And she wanted the spark. She wanted the fire. She wanted that all-consuming blaze of passion.

Of course, she could not be sure if such passion truly existed outside the marbleboard covers of the novels she had secretly devoured while still a young girl. Of a certainty, she had never seen it in the respectably married couples of Wiltshire. For all she knew, it was all a hum—a hoax to swell the subscriptions to the lending libraries.

Perhaps no living, breathing man ever loved one woman so completely that a lifetime was not sufficient to slake his thirst for her. And perhaps no real-life woman ever loved a man so deeply that to be without him was to tear a piece of her heart from her breast. But that was what Emaline wanted. And nothing less would suffice.

"I was convinced that Frank Goodman and I would not suit. And truth to tell, once he had learned to know me better—me and my managing ways—I believe he was more than happy to have his offer refused."

"Well, now, Miss Emaline, no point in wrapping an unpleasant truth in clean linen. You are a mite inclined to want to do things your own way."

"A mite," Emaline agreed with a smile.

As Pegeen carefully removed items from the workbox and laid them on the coverlet at the foot of the simple four-poster bed with its muted green and gold striped hangings, Emaline left the little lacquered settee and drew near to have a better look. Intrigued by the collection of pins, thimbles, scissors, and cards of sewing and embroidery thread, she began to look through the assortment to see if there were some small memento of her mother she might take with her.

"Perhaps there is another man you could fancy," Pegeen offered.

"No. As you said before, when a woman reaches seven and twenty . . ." She let her voice trail off. No point in reiterating the obvious.

"Are you telling me you've given up all hope of marriage, then?"

"I think perhaps I have."

Emaline mentally reviewed the three or four gentlemen who had paid particular attention to her in the past few years. Though she could recall their individual names, all the faces seemed to meld into one, and that one a facsimile of Frank Goodman's. She sighed. Barring destitution and the threat of imminent starvation, she would prefer spinsterhood to a lifetime of passionless boredom.

"But think on it, lass. Marriage is a woman's natural state. 'Tis heaven's plan for the female sex."

"Possibly, but I think the plan is not for me."

"The saints bless us! Have you no wish, then, for a man of your own to protect you?"

Emaline considered the question. "Not protect. Though I should . . ." She paused, then after a moment's reflection, she decided to confide a little in the woman who was both servant and friend. "I should like to know how it feels to be loved by a man. I would hate to miss that entirely."

Pegeen's plump cheeks grew red with indignation. "Love and a ring on the finger go together, miss, and don't you be forgetting that! Though it's a fine chance you'll have of finding either spending your days in shabby-genteel employ—"

The older woman fell silent, her hand deep inside the velvet bag that hung beneath the box. "What's this?" she asked, her voice hushed with surprise. Her dark eyes widened with amazement as she withdrew a rectangular jeweler's box, the black leather dry and cracked with age.

The lid creaked as she opened it. She gasped. "Mother of God!" she said, crossing herself with her free hand.

Startled, Emaline took the leather box from Pegeen's unresisting fingers and turned it so she could view its contents. "Oh," she whispered, every bit as awed as the older woman had been.

Fastened to the white satin lining, now yellowed with age, was a magnificent gold filigree necklace containing no less than fifteen blood-red rubies, one suspended from the center like a giant teardrop, with seven round rubies traveling to right and another seven to the left until they reached the heavy gold clasp at the back. Emaline touched the center stone with the tip of her finger, then snatched her hand back as though the gem had been hot. "Where did this come from?" she asked, her mind awhirl. "It must be worth a fortune. Father could never have purchased such a necklace. Never."

As she turned the box toward the light to get a better look at the rubies, a piece of paper fluttered to the ground, falling silently to the worn Turkey carpet. Bending down, Emaline retrieved the single sheet. The sealing wax that had once held it closed was crumbled with age. The ink was faded, but the words were yet readable, written in neat copperplate.

My very dear Jane,

I am all too aware of your sentiments upon the subject of borrowing, and for the most part, those feelings do you honor. For the sake of the pleasure it would give me, however, I pray you will suspend your principles this once and allow me to lend you these rubies. They will look wonderful with your blue silk. I want you to outshine all the society matrons when Josiah takes you to London. After all, one celebrates one's thirtieth birthday but once.

I found the necklace quite by accident, while searching through the safe for some papers. I am persuaded that Lord Seymour means the jewelry as a surprise for our wedding anniversary later this summer, but since he has ventured upon a sudden trip to the Continent, he will never know I have discovered his secret.

Do not worry about returning the rubies, for I hope to visit you again in a few weeks. I would have brought them to you myself, but there is influenza in the village. I would not risk the health of your pre-

cious Emaline by possibly exposing her. Scarcely a family in Lyle has not been stricken. I hope Bartholsby has been spared.

Until I see you again, I am reminded that old friends are the true jewels of life.

*Your loving friend,
Honoria*

Trying not to think about the epidemic of influenza that claimed her mother's life, Emaline turned the letter over to read the engraving upon the stationery. The only address was: Seymour Park, near Lyle, Wiltshire.

The paper in Emaline's hand shook. Oddly, she was disturbed as much by the discovery that her mother had a life and friends about which she knew nothing, as she was by the realization that a valuable piece of jewelry had been borrowed seventeen years ago and never restored to its owner. And how strange that the letter writer never came for the rubies, nor requested their return.

"Pegeen? Do you know a Lady Seymour? From Lyle?"

The woman began to shake her head but stopped herself. "Wait now. There was a lady something-or-other who visited your ma from time to time when you were but a wee lass. School chums, I believe they were. But I disremember the visitor's name. Don't believe I ever saw her after your sainted mother went to heaven. Is the letter from her ladyship?"

"Yes. The necklace belongs to her. Strange, do you not think, that she never asked Papa for its return."

"Sure and maybe she had so many jewels she forgot about these."

Emaline chose not to dignify that observation with a reply. Instead, she put the note back where she found it, closed the lid, and put the leather case inside the large pocket of the apron she wore. "Georgie wanted to reach the coaching inn with plenty of time to spare. Now I am glad he did, for I think I will ask the innkeeper if he can direct me to Seymour Park. If it is within walking distance of the inn, I mean to return the necklace in person. I would feel much more comfortable delivering it myself than sending it by post."

It wanted fifteen minutes until six when Emaline reached the end of the curving driveway that led to the once-elegant Palladian-style country house she hoped was indeed Seymour Park. The innkeeper had assured her the park was an easy three-mile walk, but now that she could see the uncared-for house, she was not certain she had followed his directions properly. Nor was there anyone about the place to ask for verification.

The lodge at the entrance gate was empty, and judging from the broken windows and missing thatch in the roof, no one had lived there for some time. As well, the driveway was rutted and in dire need of regrading. And if Lord Seymour employed a gardener to tend the park, the man was sadly shirking his post, for the lawn was nearly all weeds, and where topiary had once beautified the walled garden to the left of the house, now there stood only overgrown, shapeless shrubs choked with nettle.

A few white daisies and a scattering of scarlet pimpernel tried what they could to brighten the front entrance of the mansion. Unfortunately, their attempt was doomed to failure by the overpoweringly gloomy effect of decades' worth of ivy. The vines climbed the once-handsome brick facade, and in their race up the three stories to the tiled roof, they obscured a number of the front windows.

The owner must spend a fortune on candles, Emaline decided, for the ivy would render the dozen or so rooms at the front of the house dark for most of the day. Reminding herself that the owner's expenditures were no concern of hers—no more so than the darkness of the rooms or the state of the driveway—she squared her shoulders and approached the house.

"Your only concern," she said, "should be finding Lady Seymour at home."

Of course, even if her ladyship were in residence, it did not necessarily follow that she would grant an interview with an unknown visitor. She need not do so, of course. And in truth, Emaline began to hope she would not, because she must be back at the coaching inn by eight o'clock. The royal mail waited for no one.

Emaline need only assure herself that the mistress of the house was at home, then she could ask the butler to see that the box was delivered into her ladyship's hands. Content with this plan, she lifted the brass knocker and let it fall. It was necessary to knock several more times before the door was finally opened by a butler whose age and outdated attire perfectly matched the unkempt appearance of the house.

Dressed in brown knee-britches and a flared coat, he wore a haphazardly donned peruke, unpowdered, and though the wig might have looked splendid thirty years earlier, now it looked like nothing so much as an animal run over by a heavy carriage. The old man peered myopically at Emaline. "Yes?" he said finally.

"Is this Seymour Park?"

"More red hair," he muttered.

"Excuse me?" When he made no reply, Emaline decided on the instant that she could not entrust the rubies to this shrivelled and possibly senile old man. "I have come to see Lady Seymour. Please tell her I am the daughter of the Reverend Josiah Harrison."

"Her ladyship be gone."

"Gone?" Unsure if this was a euphemism, Emaline asked cautiously, "Are you telling me that Lady Seymour is dead?"

He nodded, though he had difficulty stilling the motion once he had done so. "Took by the influenza, she was, near seventeen years ago."

Emaline felt her lips quiver at the mention of influenza. Lady Seymour must have succumbed to the same epidemic that took Jane Harrison. Therein must lie the explanation for the necklace not having been reclaimed.

Obviously considering his duties at an end, the butler slowly turned away and would have closed the door if Emaline had not stepped forward and placed both her hands upon the heavy oak. "What of Lord Seymour?" she said. "Is your master at home?"

"The master rode out this afternoon."

"And will he return soon, do you think? I have something that belongs to him. Something I wish to return to his lordship personally."

"Very well," the old man replied, moving aside so she could enter. "May as well wait in the saloon with the others."

The others? Was his lordship entertaining?

Reticent to burst in upon a party of visitors, Emaline paused, fully cognizant of the impropriety of an unescorted female entering a house occupied solely by a male. She knew the guests would speedily label her as *fast;* however, her wish to return the necklace kept over-long by her family outweighed her reservations about being caught in a single gentleman's home.

Squaring her shoulders, Emaline followed the butler through the gloomy hall with its dark wainscoting and its heavy, outdated furniture. After he indicated a door to the left, the old man bent forward an inch or two in a gesture that might have been meant as a bow, then he continued toward the back of the house, leaving Emaline to enter the saloon unannounced.

If her entrance was a surprise to the two inhabitants of the room, their dissimilar appearances were a shock to her. Sitting in the grand saloon—a domed apartment with an ornate plaster ceiling from which hung numerous gossamer veils of cobwebs—was a slight, timid-looking gentleman and a startlingly flashy woman with a more than ample bosom.

The gentleman, a curate if Emaline had ever seen one—and as a rector's daughter she had met at least a dozen—wore unrelieved black. The woman—the *person*, Pegeen would have said—was arrayed in a three-quarter pelisse of orange taffeta worn over a frock of jonquil sarcenet. Her ensemble was further brightened by an amazing neckpiece of gold-dyed swansdown and an orange quilled bonnet whose shallow poke allowed two springy sausage ringlets to rest against her rouged cheeks.

Emaline tried not to stare at the ringlets, which were dyed an orange that very nearly matched the pelisse, but she was unable to stop herself from noticing the liberal application of lip salve or the heavily blackened eyelashes.

Spying Emaline, the woman put her hands on her hips, her impatience ill concealed. "It ain't his lordship," she said, glancing at the curate as though it were his fault the owner of the house was not there to greet her, "and me waiting this hour and more. Without me tea, I might add. I'm beginning to think this here trip was all a hum."

Unsure if she were expected to reply to this speech, Emaline opened her mouth to utter some platitude, but she was spared the trouble by the intervention of the curate.

"Thank heaven!" he said, ignoring the woman with the orange hair as though she did not exist, and rushing to greet Emaline the instant she stepped inside the room. "Please tell me," he begged, "that you are the young lady who is to be married this day, for I cannot in good conscience perform a ceremony in which—"

Whatever he had meant to say, his protest was cut short by a commotion in the hall. After a loud banging, caused by the front door being thrown open and hitting against the wall, three men and a youth—each of them wearing workmen's smocks—entered the house, struggling under the considerable weight of a middle-aged man who lay upon a stile gate. The gentleman's arms were folded across his chest, his face had a deathly pallor, and blood gushed from a deep gash on the side of his head.

"Lord Seymour!" the curate cried.

After one horrified peek at the injured man, he stepped back, his face almost as pale as his lordship's and his handkerchief pressed to his lips as if to stop himself from being unwell.

On the instant, the woman in the orange pelisse pushed her way past Emaline, took one look at the man lying upon the stile gate, then shrieked dramatically and fell to the floor in a swoon.

By that time, the aged butler had returned to the hall. Unfortunately, his contribution to the scene consisted of wringing his wrinkled hands and muttering, "Oh, my. Oh, my," which convinced Emaline that it was time someone brought order to the chaos.

"Here," she said, handing the man nearest the wound her clean handkerchief. "Press this firmly against the gash; it will help to stop the bleeding. You need not worry about hurting him, for I believe he is unconscious."

"Yes, miss." Lowering his voice the man added, "Wouldn't feel it nohow, like as not. Fair jug-bitten, he is, if you get my meaning." Then, obviously reconsidering the advisability of his comment, he explained that they had found his lordship in a field near the miller's property. "Must've tried to jump that old stone wall. A thing not easy to do in the best of times. No sign of his horse, but some of the lads be looking for the beast. Thought we'd best waste no time bringing his lordship home to his own bed."

"I am persuaded you did the proper thing," Emaline said. However, after glancing up the curving staircase, she became convinced that getting Lord Seymour to his bedroom would inflict unnecessary pain, no matter how inebriated he might be. "Perhaps it would be best, for the moment, to carry him into the dining room. But do not attempt to remove him from the gate. Place him, gate and all, upon the table."

Turning to the butler, she said, "Show us which is the dining room, then go to the kitchen and fetch hot water and clean towels for your master. After that, you might take a glass of something restorative to the curate. I believe he is unwell."

No one questioned her right to give orders, and as soon as the unconscious man was safely settled upon the table, Emaline turned to the youth, a likely looking lad of about fifteen summers. "Is there a doctor nearby, or an apothecary?"

The lad snatched off his cap. "Yes, missus. Mr. Vonne, the 'pothecary, be in the village."

"Will you be so kind as to fetch him here? I believe his lordship's injuries are quite serious and will require the skills of an expert."

Pulling his forelock politely, the lad fairly dashed out the door, nearly knocking over an elderly woman attired in the black dress of a housekeeper and wearing an apron and mobcap. She carried an enormous stack of folded towels. Following close behind the elderly woman was a youngish maid-of-all-work who carried a brass pitcher and a battered tin basin.

"Set them here," Emaline said, indicating a chair that had been pushed aside to allow the men access to the table.

While the maid poured steaming water into the basin, Emaline thanked the men for their services and asked if they would wait outside in case she needed them again. Obviously happy to escape, they made hasty retreats.

"You want we should go, miss?" the maid asked hopefully. "I b'aint no good with sick folks."

One look at the elderly housekeeper, whose gaze darted from the floor to the ceiling and back again—any place but at her master—convinced Emaline that she too was unable to cope with the situation. Without giving it further thought, Emaline removed her serviceable blue pelisse and bonnet and laid them on a chair well removed from the table and from harm's way. Then, hoping to protect her dove-gray kerseymere traveling dress, she took a towel from the stack, wrapped it around her waist, and pinned it behind her back with the help of the gold brooch she always wore at her neck.

After one deep breath, which did not calm her as much as she had hoped, she cautiously removed the now-bloody handkerchief from the wound. Discovering that the bleeding had been stanched, she dipped a towel into the hot water, squeezed it out, then began to cleanse the wound, touching it as gently as possible. She had only just begun the task when she heard someone enter the room, his booted steps echoing loudly on the uncarpeted floor.

The footsteps halted suddenly and a deep, masculine voice demanded, "What in blazes is going on here?"

Chapter 2

Emaline jumped as though she had been caught committing a reprehensible act. Then, already nervous, she replied more sharply than she had meant to do. "The answer to your question should be obvious."

Reaching for a fresh towel, she turned her head just far enough to discover a tall, slender gentleman with blond hair and the bluest eyes she had ever seen—a color so intense it put to shame the corbeau of the well-cut coat he wore over skin-tight, biscuit-colored pantaloons. Her first impression, after the shock of those compelling eyes, was of authority; her last, before she hurriedly looked away, was of a strange, unfamiliar flutter in that area beneath her ribs.

Continuing in a slightly more civil tone, she said, "Lord Seymour is gravely injured, and if I am to be of any help to him, it will require my complete attention. Therefore, unless you are the apothecary, I should appreciate it if you would go away."

She might as well have saved her breath, for the gentleman gave little heed to her words, choosing instead to step closer, stopping on the opposite side of the dining table as if to observe what she was doing. Though he said nothing to dissuade her from continuing her ministrations, his handsome face was set in lines of disapproval.

"I am not the apothecary," he said, "but even so, I find myself disinclined to be ordered from the room. Furthermore, I believe I figure as the patient's closest relative. Unless, of course," he continued, his tone insolent, "you have managed to outmaneuver that other redhead and have succeeded in becoming the new Lady Seymour."

Familiar with the unthinking rudeness sometimes voiced by those witnessing a loved one's pain, Emaline pressed her lips together to keep her own impolite words from spilling over. "To my knowledge, sir, there is no Lady Seymour. My name is Emaline Harrison. *Miss* Harrison."

He inclined his head, the merest suggestion of a bow, while his eyes took her full measure. Emaline pretended not to notice as slowly, insolently, he looked her over, his gaze first resting upon her face, then sliding down her neck to pause at her bosom where the tightly pinned towel pulled the soft kerseymere of her dress embarrassingly snug.

"I suppose," he said, his tone as insultingly familiar as his appraisal, "that your . . . shall we say, *friends,* call you Emma. Or do you answer to *Red?*"

Emaline caught her breath, feeling her temper flare. This was passing the line indeed. "What my friends call me is no concern of yours!"

Liam watched the burst of anger tint the woman's cheeks with rose, warming the cool, alabaster of her complexion, and for just a moment he wondered how that clear, translucent skin would feel beneath his palm.

Whoa! he told himself. Touchable skin had no business intruding upon his thoughts. If he was feeling such stirrings for the kind of courtesan who would agree to come to his cousin's house in the company of a street bawd, it meant only one thing—that he had been too long without female companionship.

The woman was not even especially beautiful. At least, not in the conventional sense. Her mouth was a bit too wide, and her nose was a touch too thin.

And yet, on closer observation her looks offered something more than mere prettiness. Her face was arresting. It was the kind a man did not easily forget. Liam supposed it had to do with her eyes—some indefinable quality in their depths. Large and brown, they were not that yellowish mixture society referred to as topaz, but a true brown. Warm and rich as sable. And trusting as a fawn's.

Trusting? What on earth had put that idea in his head? She was a woman of the demimonde. Women of her stamp learned early to trust only in what they could take to the bank. In that, she was probably no different from any other of her ilk.

Even as that thought found space in his brain, some instinct deep inside Liam told him it was not true. She was a courtesan, true enough—otherwise, why would she be in a gentleman's house without so much as a maid to lend her respectability?—but the woman who stood before him was not to be linked with the likes of that orange-haired doxy he had seen enacting a Cheltenham drama in the saloon.

Whoever she was, Emaline Harrison was no bawd from the stews. She was modestly—if not modishly—dressed, and her speech and manners were definitely refined. At one time, at least, she must have been a lady. How she had come to be a soiled dove, and under what circumstances she had chosen this life, he could only guess.

"Ohhh," Lord Seymour moaned, capturing Liam's attention.

As though the task required great effort, the patient opened his eyes. And while he tried to focus on the woman who stood above him, ministering to him, he lifted his hand toward the wound that was the source of his pain.

"Please," she said calmly, catching his hand and returning it to his chest, "do not try to move, sir. You have sustained an injury, but you are in your home and Mr. Vonne is even now on his way to attend you."

The patient seemed suddenly to become aware that someone stood on his other side. Slowly he turned his head enough to bring Liam's face into focus. When he recognized his cousin, his fleshy lips formed into an ugly sneer. "You," he muttered contemptuously.

"Cousin Ambrose," Liam replied evenly, executing a deep, mocking bow.

Returning his gaze to the woman, Lord Seymour lifted his hand again, only this time he reached up and captured a lock of shining, coppery hair that had come loose from its confining figure-eight. He yanked at the tress, forcing her face close to his. "Marry me," he ordered, his voice a raspy whisper. "Now!"

Shock registered in her lovely eyes. "My lord," she said, "you are delirious."

"But it is out of the question!" Emaline informed him stoutly, and not for the first time. "Totally preposterous!"

Politely but purposefully, Liam took her arm and led her to the top of the saloon, to a secluded corner away from the scandalized face of the curate and the belligerent stare of Mr. Boris Chapman, Lord Seymour's man of business. "The idea may be preposterous, Emma, but if it is out of the question, it is only because you refuse to listen to reason."

Emaline bristled. *"Miss Harrison,* to you. And I flatter myself that I am always reasonable."

"Good," he replied, ignoring her hauteur, "then be so

now. You have much to gain from agreeing to this proposal, and I give you my word, you have nothing to lose."

"On that point, sir, we must agree to disagree."

Liam only just controlled his exasperation. He would have understood the aversion any gently bred female must have felt at the suggestion she marry a man she had only just met—moreover, a man who, according to the apothecary, would not survive the night—but this unexpected display of reluctance on Emaline's part was ill timed. The situation did not allow Liam time for standing upon ceremony. Nor did it allow her time for pretending an overniceness of sensibilities.

His cousin's valet, Vernon Brofton, a weasel-faced man with black, angry eyes, had spent the better part of the afternoon in the local pub; it was there he had heard of his master's accident. Thus informed, he took it upon himself to fetch Lord Seymour's solicitor before returning to the park. To say the least, the twosome's reading of the situation was biased.

"Quite mysterious," the solicitor had said, innuendo dripping from every syllable. He pushed his thick spectacles back up to the bridge of his long, thin nose. "Truly baffling. At least that is what the locals are saying. So happy as they are to be in possession of a fresh tidbit of news to share with their neighbors over a pint of home brew."

"His lordship has jumped that wall a hundred times," the valet said, "with never a cut nor scrape to show for it. The villagers know that. That's the one thing they all agree on, what a bruising rider he is."

Looking about him to make certain he had the attention of the other inhabitants of the room, Brofton hinted rather broadly that he too found it odd that his master should sustain a mortal injury. " 'Specially at the very moment his cousin—his *sworn enemy*—chooses to enter the neighborhood."

"I am persuaded Major Whitcomb's arrival was mere coincidence," Chapham said, his tone giving the lie to his words.

"Coincidence, my eye," the valet muttered. "Any bloke who's got his wits about him would wonder if the major had got wind of his lordship's coming nuptials. If so, maybe he decided to do whatever it needed to stop the wedding."

Liam remained calm, refusing to rise to the bait. However, he was more concerned than he let on, keenly aware that the valet's thinly veiled accusation might not remain in this room, and that it could well be taken up by others.

While the members of the *ton* were every bit as rapacious in their desire for fresh gossip as were the workmen in the pub, they were less forgiving. More than one young woman's reputation had been ruined overnight on the strength of unfounded whispers. And though the hint of foul play might do no more than lend an air of mystery to Liam, possibly making him an object of romantic fantasies, it would put "paid" to his sister's chances.

For that reason, Liam decided it was in his family's best interest that Ambrose Whitcomb marry someone—*anyone*—before he died. If a large sum of money were required to keep the new Lady Seymour from showing herself in town and ruining his sister's come-out, it was a price he was willing to pay.

Unfortunately, getting his lordship married was not as easy as it might have been earlier in the day, especially since the number of bridal candidates had been reduced by one. The doxy with the orange hair was, at the moment, laid upon a bed in one of the upstairs rooms, drunk as a sailor newly arrived in port.

Thanks to Emaline's instructions to the butler to serve the curate a restorative, a bottle of brandy had been taken to the saloon. The still-queasy curate had declined strong spirits in preference to a cup of tea, but the orange-haired female had felt no such reserve. It seemed that her own spirits had revived as she diminished those in the bottle, until she had helped herself, quite good-naturedly, to the last drop of brandy.

When Liam and Emaline left Lord Seymour in the hands of the apothecary and returned to the front room, they discovered the doxy sprawled across the sofa, her mouth drooping open and her painted face gone slack. Once her snores became too loud to allow for normal conversation between the other inhabitants of the saloon, the valet had tossed her over his shoulder and carried her upstairs.

"Emma . . . Miss Harrison," Liam said, his voice low so the others could not hear, "I saw how gently you ministered to my cousin, and I believe you to be a kindhearted woman. For that reason, I ask that you allow me to explain why I came here today. Please."

No less susceptible to an amiably worded request than any other woman, especially when the plea came from a gentleman of both looks and address, Emaline agreed. "As you wish, sir."

Training his too-serious gaze upon her, he said, "It was not for myself I came, but for my sister. She is a very young lady, and one who is still trying valiantly to come to terms with the recent loss of our father."

At this last piece of information, Emaline knew a moment of fellow-feeling both for the young lady and for the major. She knew the pain of losing a beloved father. Despite her resolve, she felt herself weakening.

"Cordia deserves a chance at happiness," Liam continued. "A chance to be young and carefree. If the rumor is bandied about that I killed Ambrose to stop him from marrying, my sister's chances for an honorable establishment will be ruined."

He took Emaline's hand, holding it between both of his, the warmth of his touch sending its own pleading up her arm. His voice was tantalizing in its gentleness. "Can you not find it in your heart to help a young girl?"

"Sir," Emaline said, her eyelids closed to shield her thoughts from scrutiny, "you do not play fair."

Liam only just stopped the corners of his mouth from turning up in a smile. She was no fool, this courtesan with the trusting eyes.

He had not, of course, been altogether sporting, for as a soldier he had been trained to read his adversaries, a necessity for survival. The woman had no such training. She might know the ways of love, but he knew the ways of war. And he meant to win this battle. Naturally, he would see that she profited handsomely from allowing herself to be won over.

Schooling his lips not to smirk, lest she doubt his sincerity, he prodded gently, "Then you will do as I ask?"

Her eyes flew open. "I did not say that! I . . ."

Liam waited. Watching her. Allowing her to convince herself. If he knew anything of people, and he did, the argument going on inside her head would be more persuasive than any he could devise.

After a few moments quiet deliberation, she looked up at him, gazing with a forthrightness he found both refreshing and just a touch disconcerting. "Even if I should agree to this preposterous plan, Major—and believe me, that is not a strong possibility—you must know that the wedding would not be legal without a proper license. My father was the rector of St. Andrew's, at Bartholsby, and for that reason, I know about the legal requirements of a special license. For one thing, the document must be used within ninety days of its issuance."

A parson's daughter? The devil take it; she *had* come down in the world.

"In addition," she continued, "the names of the applicants, once entered on the paper, cannot be altered in any way."

"Sir!" Liam said, raising his voice so the curate could hear him. "Are you in possession of the license?"

The solicitor intercepted the question, answering suspiciously. "I have it. Why do you ask?"

Escorting Emaline back to the bottom of the room, Liam pulled up a lyre-back armchair for her. When she was settled, he asked Mr. Chapham if the names had been filled in on the document.

"See for yourself," he replied. From the inside pocket of his mulberry coat, the man removed a folded paper and held it toward Liam, who opened the crisp sheet and hurriedly read the names.

"It is filled in," Liam said, his voice not quite disguising the disappointment he felt.

Emaline relaxed against the hard back of the chair, disengaging her tightly laced fingers from their death grip. "So," she said, "that is an end to it. I am sorry for your troubles, Major Whitcomb, but I believe that we are sometimes relieved of difficult decisions by the intervention of heaven. I was reared to put my trust in such occurrences. If it had been the Almighty's will that I marry your cousin, the way would have been provided."

The solicitor smiled in self-satisfaction. "Right you are, miss. It was surely the hand of Providence that led me to discover the name of the . . . er, prospective bride before I procured the license. And though I forgot her last name, the clerk agreed it would be legally binding with only the name by which she is called."

Emaline looked at the major's unreadable face. "I truly regret—" She stopped, the words catching in her throat, for the solicitor continued to speak.

"Agnes," he said. "A plain, old-fashioned name, to be sure, but legal for all that."

Emaline gasped. With a hand that was far from steady, she touched the initialed brooch she had refastened to the neck of her dress only minutes ago. Fate seemed to move her forefinger, bidding it trace the ornately engraved *H* in the center, the *E* on the right, then the *A* on the left.

Major Whitcomb was watching her, his dark blue eyes practically burning a hole in the brooch. "A pretty piece," he said quietly. "An heirloom?"

Unable to form the words of denial, Emaline merely shook her head. The major's look was so knowing, so confident that she knew there was no point in trying to hide the evidence.

"*Your* initials?" he asked.

She nodded.

He smiled, revealing beautiful, even teeth. "I believe you were saying something about putting your trust in heavenly intervention."

Chapter 3

"The gentlemen be returning from the funeral, your ladyship."

Emaline blushed guiltily, as she did every time someone called her by her new title. "Thank you, Betsy. Please inform Major Whitcomb that I wish to speak with him at his earliest convenience."

The maid curtsied and left the saloon, closing the door behind her.

Lady Seymour. Married.

Emaline still could not believe she had acted with such disregard for the proprieties. If Pegeen were here now, what would she say? And Papa! Dear Papa would be appalled. Of course, it was a bit late to be wondering what anyone might say upon the subject, because the deed, rash as it was, had been done. It could not be undone.

As had happened so many times these last two days, Emaline experienced again that hollow feeling in the pit of her stomach, that sense of having been caught in a web of her own making. Following the revelation that the only name written on the license was Agnes—her own middle name—she had felt like a pawn of fate.

The hour that followed had seemed more like a dream

than reality. A dream in which she was three parts observer and only one part participant.

Once the major had convinced the curate that he had heard Ambrose ask Emaline to marry him, they had all gone to the dining room, where Mr. Vonne attested to the fact that his lordship had regained consciousness only moments earlier and that he was quite agitated, asking for his bride. Though still not happy with the circumstances, the curate was finally persuaded to conduct the ceremony, with the apothecary and the housekeeper serving as witnesses.

The bride's responses were no less feeble than the groom's. When all questions had been asked and answered, and Lord Seymour's heavy signet ring placed upon Emaline's finger, the couple were pronounced husband and wife. " 'Til death shall ye part."

Emaline had quit the room the moment the pronouncement was made, and not until the next morning, after a fitful sleep, was she informed that her new husband had not survived the night. The only bright spot in the entire affair had been the information imparted by Betsy, the maid who brought her can of hot water, that the prevailing practice in the neighborhood was for the widow of the deceased to absent herself from the burial.

How quickly Emaline had seized upon that custom as her excuse for eschewing the funeral service. As well, she declined the rusty black dress the housekeeper had offered as proper for her to wear, refusing to mourn a man she never knew. "I have made a mockery of the wedding vows, but I will not insult those whom I have truly mourned by a sham display for a stranger."

Not even Major Whitcomb's added voice had convinced her to don the black.

Major Whitcomb. Emaline sighed. She had been a bit

foolish there; she realized that now. A smile, a few softly spoken words from the man, and she had acted more like a green girl than a woman in control of her life.

Control? What an absurd piece of self-deception.

A woman in control would not have allowed herself to be lured into cooperating with Liam simply because he paid her a bit of attention. Such a woman would have ignored that way he had of listening with his head angled ever so slightly to the side, giving the impression of total absorption in the speaker's words. A more determined woman would have disregarded that breathlessness she felt when he had held her hand within the warmth of his. If she had been in control, they never would have reached the point where the name upon the license was revealed. At that instant, there was no going back.

Weary with repining over something that could not be changed, Emaline was happy when her unproductive thoughts were interrupted by a knock at the saloon door. At her answer, the door was opened and the new Baron Seymour stepped inside the room.

Liam was dressed in black, as befitted a gentleman attending the funeral of a relative, but far from causing him to look somber, the clothes accentuated his own vivid coloring. The black coat and britches, contrasting with the pristine whiteness of his shirt and neckcloth, emphasized the blondness of his straight, thick hair and the vibrant blue of his eyes.

Standing there, with the fresh, clean aroma of the out-of-doors clinging to him, he was earth . . . and sky . . . and sun.

At a distance of some eighteen feet, Emaline could feel the energy of all three elements, and as he relaxed his elegant person against the door frame, the feeling seemed to intensify rather than diminish.

Because she could not avert her gaze without appearing missish, she studied Liam in his relaxed pose, his shoulder pressed against the door and one booted foot crossed over the other. Leisurely she regarded each feature, taking special notice of his broad shoulders, his strong thighs, and his muscular calves.

His body was long, and lean . . . and beautiful. No other word for it. So beautiful the mere sight of it left her spellbound.

"Handsome as he can stare," Agnes had called him.

Before the woman had left to catch the mail coach to London, she had informed Emaline that the major was an exceedingly wealthy man. Still indisposed from her injudicious consumption of brandy, Agnes had been unable to travel the next day, and was obliged to spend a second night at Seymour Park. A gregarious sort, she had needed less than a day to get to know all the inmates of the house, and had gleaned from them some quite interesting bits of gossip.

"According to the servants," Agnes had confided, her friendly tone implying that she was not one to hold a grudge simply because she had missed out on being the new Lady Seymour, "when the major's old da put his spoon in the wall, he left his son richer by close to a million pounds. Cooee! Can you believe it?"

Emaline had been speechless.

"He's what the toffs call a *premier parti,* he is. What with him being rich as can be, not to mention handsome as he can stare, it wants only time enough for the word to get around that he's a lordship, and the London ladies will be trying every trick in the book to get him to toss the handkerchief their way."

Looking at him now, Emaline had to agree with Agnes's

prediction. Even without the added inducement of wealth, any woman must find Liam Whitcomb a desirable *parti*.

"You wished to speak with me about something?" he asked.

His words broke the spell, and Emaline was thankful to be able to call her unruly mind back to order. She'd had no idea she could react so to a man's physique. "Actually," she said somewhat shakily, "there are two matters I wish to discuss."

He angled his head slightly, giving her his full attention. "I am listening."

"Now that the obsequies have been observed, I wish to leave Seymour Park as soon as possible. The letter to my employer, which your valet posted for me when he took Agnes to catch the mail coach, explained only that I would be delayed a day or so. I do not wish to alienate Mrs. Zuber by delaying my arrival overlong."

Liam straightened away from the wall, his ease of a moment earlier gone. *Her employer*. The very thought of her worrying about inconveniencing some vile *abbess* made him crave to draw someone's cork.

"You promised to make the arrangements for my travel," she continued, "and I shall hold you to that pledge."

"It shall be as you wish," he replied, his voice cool, "but not today. Mrs. Zuber must exercise patience a bit longer, for there are a few things we need to discuss before you take your leave. For the moment, however, I believe you said there were *two* items you wished to speak to me about."

"Yes. The first item was my travel arrangements. The second is this." From atop the pie-crust table beside the wing chair in which she sat, she retrieved a worn leather jeweler's box. Holding it toward him, she said, "You were busy most of yesterday, else I would have given it to you earlier."

Liam strolled to within a few feet of her chair. "What is this?" he asked, glancing at the object but making no move to take it from her hand. "Have females embraced some new custom since I left for the Continent? I do not recall ever having been on the receiving end of a jeweler's box."

She blushed a most becoming rose. "It is not a gift, sir. It is my reason for being here."

"Your reason for . . . Do you mean *here*, at Seymour Park?"

"Yes."

"Forgive me, I must be woefully dense this morning, for I am afraid I do not understand your meaning. You came at my cousin's invitation, did you not? To witness the wedding between him and your friend."

She shook her head. "How could I? I knew nothing of Agnes until two days ago, when I entered this house. Nor had I ever met his lordship. I came for only one reason, to return this jewelry to Lady Seymour. Since both she and her husband are deceased, I am persuaded that you must now be the rightful owner."

Curious, Liam reached for the box, opened it, then glanced at its contents. It was with no little difficulty that he hid his surprise at the sight of the brilliant red necklace pinned to the bed of yellowed satin. Schooling his voice to a degree of calmness he did not feel, he asked, "How did this come to be in your possession?"

"I found it two days ago, while packing my father's personal things. The new rector was due to arrive the following day, and I—"

"The new rector?" Liam felt like a man who had arrived late at the theater, and as a consequence could make neither head nor tail of the plot of the play being enacted on the stage.

"I told you," she said slowly, as though explaining something to one who understood only foreign tongues, "that my father was rector of St. Andrew's at Bartholsby. While I was packing his possessions to be sent to the workhouse, I found the jeweler's box. There was a note inside, a note written by Lady Seymour. She had lent the necklace to my mother. Because I was on my way to London to take up my new post, I decided to return the rubies in person, and perhaps explain the delay to her ladyship."

"What post?" he fairly shouted.

"With Mrs. Zuber," she replied, "as her paid companion." Looking at him rather closely, she said, "Major, I wonder if you remained too long in the sun this morning. You seem somewhat distracted."

"Somewhat? Ma'am, I am deucedly distracted!"

After closing the leather case with a firm snap, he tossed it onto the sofa, surprising Emaline with his cavalier disregard for the ruby necklace that had, in essence, been the cause of her being embroiled in this entire episode.

"We shall discuss this later," he said, turning and striding hurriedly to the door. When his hand touched the handle, he paused, his back to her. "First, the funeral breakfast must be got through. After that, my cousin's solicitor is prepared to read the will. You may absent yourself from the breakfast, if you so choose, but for the sake of the legalities, you must be present for the reading of the last will and testament."

Emaline moaned. "Will this ordeal never be at an end?"

"A good question, ma'am." Liam turned back to her, staring at her for what seemed a long time. "A very good question. Would that I had the answer."

After promising to have the maid bring her a tray, he exited the room, closing the door softly behind him.

While Emaline waited for what she hoped would be a bracing cup of tea, she decided to take a turn around the room. She had been disinclined to venture out of doors, afraid of meeting some neighbor come to offer his condolences, but the enforced inactivity of the past two days was galling to a woman accustomed to a busy life liberally interspersed with physical exercise.

The saloon was not a room decorated to inspire admiration, and as she circled it for the third time, she wondered if anyone had used the room since her mother's friend had been in residence. Other than the gloomy atmosphere, due mainly to the ivy that obscured the leaded windows, the carpet was faded and in need of a good beating. Also, the upholstery upon the sofa and the chairs was frayed in places, with more than one broken spring lying in wait to give a nasty start to anyone unwise enough to sit before looking.

The only handsome piece of furniture in the entire saloon was a walnut vitrine that stood in a corner at the top of the room. Featuring elaborately carved *rocaille* and scrolls, the cabinet was fashioned with striking beveled glass panels, through which could be seen a half-dozen books and a few small *objets d'art*.

Deciding to stop, Emaline opened the delicate doors. The objects inside were charming, if of little value—an enameled snuff box, a glazed pottery owl, a little silver pincushion. Upon closer inspection, she noticed that in places on the shelves there were small circles and squares in the thick dust, ghostly reminders of items that had once occupied the space.

"The master sold all the good pieces," the maid said, setting a tray containing a pot of tea and a plate of sandwiches on a tripod table near the chair Emaline had just vacated. "On the top shelf, near those books that belonged to the mistress, there was used to be a sweet little China shepherdess. Wore a pretty pink dress, she did, with an old-timey blue basque, and a tall hat with streamers that fair blew in the wind. I always wanted to take it out and look at it in the light, but I was afeared I might drop it."

From the shabbiness of the house, Emaline was not surprised that Lord Seymour had resorted to selling off his wife's trinkets. Momentarily wishing she could have seen the pretty shepherdess, Emaline absently withdrew one of the slim books, blew a cloud of dust from its gold-lettered morocco cover, then carried it with her to the chair. If the guests remained long at the funeral breakfast, and the major—she must remember to call him by his new title—was delayed, at least she would have something to read while she waited. Please heaven the book would prove interesting!

As it transpired, it proved to be an extremely happy choice. Entitled *How to Attract, Captivate, and Fascinate a Member of the Male Sex*, its author was described only as Madame X, a member of the nobility. According to the frontispiece, a companion volume, *How to be Alluring to One's Husband, Or: How to Provoke Those Passions that Fade with Time*, was also in circulation.

The pair were written in the previous century—a period famous for its more relaxed mores—and the titles of the ten chapters of the first book were enough to put a modern young lady to the blush. Emaline was made of sterner stuff, however, and was soon engrossed in the opening pages of Chapter One.

In those first few pages, the reader was instructed to use

her eyes to attract a gentleman, and Emaline was only just discovering the fine distinction between eyes that smiled, those that beckoned, and those that smoldered, when Liam spoke her name, startling her into a gasp. In her haste to close the book, lest he chance to read so much as a word of it, she dropped the little volume onto the floor.

"Sir!" she gasped, embarrassment warming her face. "Must you tread so softly?"

"Your pardon, ma'am. I knocked, but you must not have heard."

Bending to retrieve the fallen book for her, Liam was more than a little surprised when she hurriedly placed her foot upon the morocco cover, obscuring the gold lettering of the title. Slowly, carefully, she drew her foot and the thin missive beneath the hem of her lilac skirt.

He thanked heaven that he had already discovered his error in believing her a courtesan. Otherwise, he might have mistaken her move as one of overt coquetry, an invitation for him to lift the hem of her skirt for a view of her ankles, on the pretext of searching out the book. Worse yet, considering the way thoughts of her softly curving figure—and especially the shape of her long limbs—had intruded upon his dreams the night before, he was very much afraid he would have been tempted to accept the invitation.

The devil take it! He had been entertaining carnal fantasies about a lady. And not just any lady. A parson's daughter.

My God! She was his cousin!

Shaken by this realization, Liam straightened, made her a polite bow, then walked over to the sofa, settling himself upon the threadbare rose damask.

While he studied her averted gaze and her still-pink cheeks, he asked himself what he was to do now. Now that he knew who she was—or, more accurately, who she was not. That question had plagued him throughout the tedious funeral breakfast. And though he had given the matter his full attention, practically ignoring the half-dozen gentlemen of the neighborhood who partook of the meal, not one logical solution had occurred to him.

Liam had meant to put her on the public stage, as he had done Agnes, so that she could return to London and to her own life. Having already made out a draft on his bank in the amount of one thousand pounds, he had intended giving it to her just before she boarded the coach, inducement for her to embrace the quiet life until his sister's season was at an end.

A *demi rep* would have smiled and accepted the very generous draft; no harm done.

But she was not a *demi rep*. She was a young lady of birth and breeding, and as such, harm had been done her. Or it would be if the nature of this marriage were discovered. If the story got out, *her* reputation would be ruined. He would have sacrificed one young lady to protect another.

And the blame was entirely his.

Ignoring her protestations, he had coerced—nay, impelled—her to agree to the wedding. When she had insisted loud and long that she could not do it, he had manipulated her, using her compassion and even her religious beliefs to trap her into agreeing to do his bidding.

He had acted unconscionably. Now he must do all within his power to protect her from his high-handedness. How that was to be accomplished he did not know. He needed time to devise a suitable plan.

To Liam's relief, the solicitor chose that moment to enter the room, several sheets of paper in his hand. "Sir. Lady

Seymour," he said, bowing to Emaline, "I hope I find you well."

Without giving her an opportunity to answer, Liam said, "Let us get on with it, sir."

While Mr. Chapham settled himself into one of the lyreback chairs, Emaline retrieved the little book from beneath her hem and slipped it into her reticule, gathering the strings tightly so the missive would be safe from discovery until she could return it to the vitrine. She supposed it was a sign of some sort that she had been caught out, for if she were truly her father's daughter, she would not have read even the first page of such a book. Vowing to rid herself of it at the first opportunity, she turned her attention to the solicitor, who had been droning on for several minutes.

"I have already informed the servants of the bequests to them," he said, "so with your permission, Major, I shall omit the list of entailed property at this time and go directly to the section pertaining to his lordship's widow."

"Widow! No. No," Emaline said, shaking her head. "This is a mistake. I do not want anything."

The solicitor stared at her over the rim of his glasses. "Perhaps you did not perfectly understand, my lady. This document was executed twenty years ago. The Lady Seymour referred to in the will was his lordship's first wife."

Emaline exhaled, then relaxed against the cushioning of the wing chair. "Thanks be to heaven."

"Although," he continued, after glancing through the remainder of the page, "her ladyship's name is not mentioned."

"It was Honoria," Emaline said, hoping the information would satisfy the oversight.

Putting the papers aside, Chapham steepled his fingers, studying the configuration as though it would help him to explain the situation. "I am not at all certain what should be done here. All entailed property goes to the next in line to the barony, in this instance Major Whitcomb, but his lordship's unentailed assets—the town house, his horses and carriage, any art or jewelry he may have purchased—are left to his wife. As there is no name stipulated, madam, this might well mean you."

"No!" Emaline jumped up from her chair and walked over to the empty fireplace, her mind awhirl at this latest predicament. "I cannot accept these things. Give them to Major Whitcomb. He is Lord Seymour now. I am persuaded Lord Sey . . . my hus . . . that is to say, *the deceased* would wish it that way."

"And I," the solicitor replied, "am persuaded he would not!"

Emaline glanced at the new Baron Seymour, hoping he would enter the discussion. He said nothing, appearing rather to be lost in thought.

"It might be," Chapham continued, "that the first Lady Seymour has relatives who would feel they have a claim against her estate. If that is the case, then you might possibly have to relinquish your own claim. Always assuming," he added with a question in his voice, "that the new Baron Seymour does not contest the will."

Liam muttered something under his breath.

"Leave a copy of the testament with Lady Seymour," he said. "When she reaches London, she may visit a solicitor of her own choosing. Someone not associated with either the eighth Baron Seymour or myself, and therefore unbiased. She can leave it to her solicitor to work out the details of the will, and, if necessary, to place the matter before the courts."

"Can you not understand?" Emaline asked, frustration

making her speak louder than she had meant to do. "I want nothing! I am entitled to nothing."

"Do not despair," Liam said, "for *nothing* may prove to be exactly what you have inherited. I believe my cousin was often heavily in debt. You may count yourself fortunate if no outstanding bills are shoved beneath your door by irate tradesmen."

Emaline gasped.

"That, too," Liam assured her pleasantly, "may be left to your solicitor to handle. As for your generous offer to hand over the entire estate to me, believe me, I had much rather you did not."

The road to London was bumpier than Emaline had imagined, but she felt certain the major's well-sprung berline made the trip much smoother than it would have been aboard the royal mail she had originally planned to take to the city. Pulled by four well-matched horses, the dark green coach fairly ate up the road, traveling at better than ten miles per hour. Since little time was lost at the posting inns where the horses were changed, it was still early afternoon when the carriage arrived at the Inn of the Fields, where she and Liam planned to rest and partake of a nuncheon.

Within minutes of her arrival, Emaline discovered that Lady Seymour was given much more distinguished attention than plain Miss Harrison would have received. Shown to a room with pretty yellow bedhangings and a small dressing table complete with a looking glass, she was divested of her pelisse and bonnet by a solicitous maid who then poured warm, lavender-scented water into the pretty China basin on the washstand. A cake of transparent soap and two pristine white towels were supplied for "m'lady's" convenience.

Refreshed as much by the stretching of her limbs as by the amenities of the bedchamber, Emaline soon joined Liam in the private dining parlor that faced onto the bustling inn yard.

In deference to the conventions, he left the door to the parlor open; then he led her across the room to a small table set with fresh linens, two place settings, and more than enough food to satisfy six ravenous guests.

"You found everything to your satisfaction abovestairs?" he asked, seating her in the chair opposite his.

"I should be hard to please if I had not found it so. Those with pure hearts may inherit the earth, Major, but I can bear witness to the fact that it is those with titles who get the best rooms at the inn."

A glint of amusement lit Liam's eyes. "So you no longer find your new name onerous, ma'am?"

"On the contrary. It grows more charming by the minute."

After unfolding the napkin and placing it on her lap, Emaline dropped a lump of sugar into her teacup and began to stir the mahogany-colored liquid. "I do not flatter myself that you will recollect this, sir, for you had much else on your mind at the time I mentioned it, but I feel quite strongly upon the subject of heavenly intervention in our lives. For this reason—"

"You are mistaken," Liam interrupted, "I do recall your sentiments upon the matter. How could I not, when they played such an important part in your becoming Lady Seymour."

"My point exactly," she said, concentrating her attention upon adding the merest drop of cream to her tea. "My father taught me that all prayers are answered. He believed that when we are not given that for which we ask, it is because that thing requested was not in our best interest. I embrace that belief and take it a step farther. When we follow an ethical course—one that will offer harm to no one—and that course is suddenly altered, I consider the alteration to be a positive answer to a prayer not yet voiced. As a result, I have learned not to struggle against the tide, but to surrender, letting the current carry me effortlessly in the direction I am meant to go."

"And this . . . this current has now led you to accept your new name?"

"It has." She lifted the cup to her lips and drank thirstily. "A few months ago I declined an offer of marriage—an offer that I had every reason to suspect would be my last. At seven and twenty, I assumed it was settled that I should remain single my entire life. I need not remind you," she said, "how quickly that assumption proved untrue."

"No. You need not remind me." His voice was low, as though he spoke more to himself than to her.

Picking up the carving knife, he sliced off a portion of ham and placed it upon her plate. "Far be it from me to cast aspersions upon your accepted tenets, but it was not the current that foisted that change in status upon you. It was I. I abused your good nature to suit my own purpose, and now is as good a time as any to beg your pardon for having embroiled you in a situation that may prove an embarrassment to you. I pray you will allow me to make what reparation I may."

Emaline waved aside his offer. "I accept your apology, sir, but only because it would be churlish of me not to do so. As for reparation, pray do not be absurd. Believe me, you were powerless to change the tide of events. As was I."

He cocked one eyebrow. "So, I am to be held totally blameless. All repercussions, good or ill, are to be laid at the door of—what was it again?—heavenly intervention."

"Exactly. How quickly you grasp these weighty metaphysical concepts."

"And how readily you choose to misunderstand me."

"Not so, Major. I understand you well enough. You are concerned for my welfare. And though the feeling does you credit, I wish you will put it from your mind. I am quite capable of taking care of myself."

"But I, and my family, owe you—"

"You owe me nothing."

To forestall further argument, she served both their plates with a spoonful of the contents of each of the four side dishes. "In surrendering to the current that swept me to Seymour Park, I have acquired a new name and title—items of inestimable value—and I have determined to enjoy them. Especially since it will suit my purpose much better to be known as a married lady."

"Your purpose? I had thought you fixed upon a career as a companion."

"That was but a means to an end; as a single lady I could not live alone." She stayed the forkful of fricasseed asparagus that was halfway to her mouth. "My purpose is to enjoy the city. To partake of its gaiety and amusements."

"An innocent enough ambition. Could you not . . ." His voice trailed off. He watched, bemused, as she placed the fricassee in her mouth, then closed her lips around the fork and drew it out . . . slowly, tantalizingly. "Er—could your goal not be accomplished as a single lady?"

"Certainly not. Unwed females are fettered about by all manner of restrictions. You must know the case is quite different for a married woman."

"I know nothing of the sort! Furthermore," he added, "I trust you will forgive my indelicacy, but you are *not* a married woman."

"A mere technicality. Moreover, it is one to which only you and I are privy."

Scooping up another bite of fricassee, she held the fork poised, very near her mouth. Liam followed its progress, unable to avert his eyes. "I am sadly tired of the rules and regulations to which maiden ladies must adhere, and now that I am Lady Seymour, those tedious restrictions need no longer apply."

He watched her put the asparagus in her mouth, exactly as she had done before. Only this time, it was much worse. He moaned inwardly as she spied a morsel that had adhered to the fork and, using the tip of her tongue, carefully licked off the errant scrap, totally unaware of the provocativeness of the act.

She is such a naive creature! Without the least notion of the baser instincts of the male sex!

And here she was talking of ignoring the rules that protected innocent females. Liam bit back a curse. Let her believe what she wished about divine intervention; he knew who was responsible for her marrying his cousin, and if some disaster befell her while playing the merry widow, it would be his fault.

A picture flashed through his mind of a certain pretty, young widow whose company and attentions he had once enjoyed. Their liaison had lasted for several months, and in that time the lady had lived in a way that was anything but *fettered*. When his regiment sailed for the Continent, the liaison had ended, but the pretty widow had discovered any number of gentlemen ready and willing to step into the breach to console her.

Prodded by this memory, Liam felt it incumbent upon him to drop Emaline a hint about the type of gentlemen who pursued young widows. Especially those widows who supposed that their having been married would afford them unlimited freedom.

"It is well to remember," he began, "that in general, the male sex are more likely to ignore the boundaries if a lady does not observe them. They may even take liberties with—"

"Liam!" shouted a uniformed gentleman who stood just outside the open doorway. "By Jove, it is you. I thought I recognized that dark green berline."

"Champ!"

Pushing his chair aside, Liam moved swiftly to the doorway, his hand extended in greeting, a warm smile upon his face. "I did not think to see you before Michelmas."

Ignoring Liam's outstretched hand, the tall, dark-haired newcomer engulfed him in a bear hug. "They let me go early," he said. "How could they not, after I won the war singlehandedly."

Laughing at his friend's foolishness, Liam freed himself from the rough embrace. Then, holding him at arm's length, he looked him up and down. "You are not wounded?"

"Not a scratch, old son. Told you I led a charmed life."

"And the regiment? How goes it with the men? Had we many losses at Waterloo?"

The gentleman's handsome face sobered for a moment, the gray eyes losing their teasing light. "It was bad," he said quietly. "Real bad. Even worse than Toulouse. We—"

Suddenly noticing that they were not alone, his friend fell silent, staring at Emaline a moment before averting his gaze. "Liam, never tell me you've been caught in parson's mousetrap."

"No, no. The lady is not my wife."

His friend glanced once again toward the table. "Well she certainly isn't Miss Cordia, for I remember you telling me she was a very young lady, close in age to my own sister."

After a moment's reflection, Captain Geoffrey Beauchamp smiled broadly, as though he had solved a riddle. Poking his elbow into his friend's rib, he winked. "Liam, you old dog, you have a ladybird in tow!"

Liam groaned, mentally discerning the strains of that piper's tune for which all must ultimately pay. The time had come to test the expurgated version of the events of the past three days. It was a version agreed upon by him and Emaline, an account whose believability would prosper or fail according to the skill of the narrators. Bowing to the inevitable, he said, "Mind your manners, Champ. The lady is my cousin."

Chapter 4

Wishing his friend had stopped anyplace but at this particular inn, Liam led him over to the table where Emaline waited.

"Ma'am," he began, "allow me to present to you a friend of long standing. Captain Geoffrey Beauchamp, of His Majesty's Hussars. Champ, I make you known to Lady Seymour."

"A pleasure, Captain," Emaline said, extending her hand.

"Lady Seymour," he replied, bowing smartly, then saluting her fingertips with a kiss, "the pleasure is entirely mine." Employing a smile Liam had seen him use to his benefit many times, the newcomer continued, "In fact, ma'am, in my prayers this evening I shall thank the gods for prompting me to pause at this inn. Without their intervention, I might never have known that Liam had a cousin whose hair rivals the sun and whose fair cheeks put roses to the blush." The words poured from his mouth as smoothly as warmed honey. "Your husband is a fortunate man."

Liam marveled that anyone could utter such treacle with a straight face. Concerned lest Emaline find the fulsome compliments distasteful, he searched her countenance for a sign that he should restrain his friend. To his dismay, a smile played at the corners of her full, soft lips.

"My husband is deceased, sir."

The reply was made with such ease that Liam suspected she had been practicing the phrase, holding it in readiness for just such an occasion as this.

"She has only just become a widow!" he added, surprising himself as well as Emaline with a revelation he had meant to keep as quiet as possible.

Far from quelling the military gentleman's gallantry, however, this information seemed rather to encourage it. "My condolences," he said, his tone anything but sympathetic.

"You are very kind, sir."

"Not at all, ma'am."

Champ put his hand on the back of Emaline's chair, his stance far too familiar to suit Liam's taste. "Since you are on this road," his friend said, "might I assume that you are traveling to town?"

"We are," she answered. "And you, sir?"

"As fortune would have it, that is my destination as well."

With that same insouciant look Liam had watched him use numerous times with other, more worldly ladies, Champ said, "Since Liam does not maintain a residence in town, and will probably not be at hand should you need an escort, I would be delighted to offer you my services during your sojourn. Any service whatsoever. You have only to ask."

"Again, sir, you are very kind."

"On the contrary," he said, smiling and lifting her hand to his lips once again, "it is you who are kind, for bestowing your lovely smile upon me."

Damne! Champ is flirting with her!

"My friendship with Liam is of such long standing, Lady

Seymour, that I am emboldened to hope that you, too, will look upon me as a friend."

This is passing all bounds! Liam was on the verge of admonishing the rascal to mind his manners, when Emaline's light laughter stilled his words.

"I have never been to town before, Captain, and as a consequence, I have no friends there."

To Liam's surprise, she looked downward for a moment, then slowly lifted her gaze until her brown eyes looked directly into Champ's gray ones. "How comfortable I will feel, knowing I may call upon a man such as you—a gentleman who has served his country with honor and valor. I shall try my wings with greater freedom knowing I may depend upon the friendship of one well versed in the ways of the world."

Devil take it! She is flirting back!

Without being invited to do so, Champ pulled up a chair for himself, placing it unconsciously close to Emaline's. "I told Liam I led a charmed life. Did I not, old son? This is Fate's handiwork, for here you are on your way to town at just the moment I am escorting my mother and sister there for the little season. When you are settled in, ma'am, may I give myself the pleasure of visiting you?"

"I should be delighted to receive you, Captain Beauchamp."

"Please. Call me Champ. Everyone does."

"Thank you, Champ. My friends call me Emaline."

It was as well for Liam's composure that his friend stayed for only a few minutes. "I trust you see what I mean," he said the moment Captain Beauchamp quit the room. "That display of careless manners quite proves my point that even the best of men cannot be relied upon to observe the boundaries if a lady grants them too much freedom."

Emaline's dreamlike smile did nothing to reassure him that she grasped the seriousness of the situation.

"Yes," she said with a sigh, "I see *just* what you mean."

The remainder of their meal, not to mention the final thirty miles to be covered before they reached London, were completed in virtual silence. Their only comments were those stiffly polite questions regarding her comfort, which Liam apparently felt impelled to ask, and the brief platitudes she employed by way of answer.

The reason for Liam's being up in the boughs, Emaline could not guess, but as near as she could estimate, his change of mood had started about the time of Captain Beauchamp's arrival. Strange, that. Who would have thought that a reunion with an old friend would put him so out of countenance?

For her part, Emaline had been quite pleased with her exchange with the handsome soldier. And regardless of what Liam said, she had granted the captain no freedoms. He had merely assumed that since she was a married lady, he could be more relaxed in her presence.

Their flirtation—to call it what was—had been delightful. She had enjoyed it immensely. Especially once she found the nerve to try that thing with the eyes.

Following the instruction of the little book she had found in the vitrine, she had lifted her gaze slowly, but with a smile in her aspect rather than a smolder. She had not the audacity to try for smoldering—not yet, at any rate. For that she needed a degree of rehearsal before her looking glass.

Actually, the innocent artifice had succeeded better than in her wildest dreams. Surprisingly, merely making the attempt had bestowed upon her a sort of power. When the captain responded to her look, Emaline felt almost giddy with success, a feeling she had not experienced since that Christmas a number of years ago when she drank four cups of her father's champagne punch.

To attract a man like Captain Beauchamp was no small accomplishment. And he had been attracted; she was not mistaken about that. Evidently a ladies' man, he was a gentleman of both charm and wit, and his darkly handsome looks had done nothing to diminish his appeal. Though not nearly as handsome as Liam, the captain possessed that quality that most females, be they young or old, found irresistible. He was an unrepentant rogue.

He is rogue! Liam thought, and I must have a talk with him as soon as possible. Geoffrey Beauchamp was his oldest and closest friend, and a man to whom he would entrust his very life, but he was a man who enjoyed the ladies. A lot. And damn his eyes, the ladies reciprocated.

But for all that, Liam remembered, Champ was a gentleman, not some defiler of innocents. Recalling this fact enabled Liam to breathe easier. A word would be sufficient to convince his friend to have a care. In a day or two, when he found the time, Liam would drop him a note explaining the circumstances of Emaline's marriage to Ambrose. Champ could be trusted to keep the story to himself, and once he knew the truth, he could be trusted to keep the line where Lady Seymour was concerned.

Comfortable with his decision, Liam was able to relax and give himself up to the soporific swaying of the coach. Glancing in Emaline's direction, he noticed that the rhythmic rocking was taking its toll upon her as well. Her eyelids had grown heavy. She was fighting the lure of sleep.

Eventually, she lost the battle and her head fell forward upon her chest.

Concerned that she might suffer a stiff neck, Liam felt compelled to do the gentlemanly thing. Untying the satin ribbons of her bonnet, he tossed the blue straw onto the opposite seat, slipped his arm around her shoulders, and guided her head to his chest.

Without waking, Emaline nestled contentedly against him, innocently searching out the spot within the hollow of his shoulder that best suited her. Fortunately, Liam suffered this delicate assault upon his person with relative composure. As well, he remained almost unruffled when a hint of lavender wafted gently from her warm skin, teasing his nostrils. He had only just finished congratulating himself upon his iron control when his calm was shaken to its very center.

Lost in the pleasure afforded him by the fragrance of her, he was unprepared for the reaction of his senses when the fine-boned hand that was beneath her cheek fell away, slipping drowsily across his chest to come to rest just inside his coat. The warmth of her fingertips fairly scorched his skin, seeming to penetrate both his marcella waistcoat and the linen of his shirt, almost as if his bare flesh were exposed to her touch. Immediately he was aware of her nearness, her warmth, and her softness.

Perhaps holding her had not been an altogether wise idea!

Turning his head slightly to relieve the sudden tightness of his collar, Liam let his chin rest upon her soft hair. That, too, was a mistake, for it brought his lips into contact with a coppery curl that had escaped the confines of its coiffure.

Without thinking, he allowed the silken tress to brush against his parted lips, even assisting it in its gentle caress by moving his mouth ever so slightly. Once. Twice. Three times. What harm could it do, one simple lock of hair? Obviously more harm than he had dreamed possible, for very soon he grew dissatisfied with that teasing sample and began to imagine not the curl but Emaline's lips brushing his.

How easy it would be to transform imagination to reality. The work of an instant. He need only shift her unresisting body so that her head rested in the crook of his arm, her face turned up to his.

His breathing grew uneven as he envisioned himself waking her with—

Devil take it! What am I doing?

Realizing what he had been thinking, Liam cursed himself for a idiot. How could he have allowed his thoughts to journey in that direction?

Foolish beyond permission!

He had as good as pledged himself to protect her from the wolves who waited in London for just such unsophisticated lambs as she, yet here he was indulging in what could only be called lascivious daydreams.

Ordering himself to get a rein on his emotions, he turned his head away abruptly. This was merely his body talking. Emaline was pressed against him, her flesh soft and pliant, and he was but a man. A healthy man. Any woman, he decided, would have aroused that same reaction in him.

Any woman.

While he enumerated the quite logical reasons for his response to her nearness, she murmured softly, and as she stirred, her arm went deeper beneath his coat until it was around his waist. Still asleep, she insinuated herself closer to him until she found the resting place she sought. With her arm around him, and the side of her soft breast pressed against his chest, Liam was forced to take several deep breaths to steady his rapidly beating pulse.

Despite his discomfort, he was loath to push her away. An officer and a gentleman, he resigned himself to the situation. Giving in as gracefully as possible, he put both his arms around her and held her close. With one booted foot braced against the opposite seat to support the two of them should the carriage encounter a stretch of bad road, he settled against the berline's well-padded velvet squab and relaxed as best he could.

In time, he too succumbed to the swaying of the coach. He closed his eyes, content to have his arms about her, happy to have her soft body against his, and completely forgetting that he was supposed to be protecting her from just such compromising positions.

Emaline came awake slowly. For a time she kept her eyes tightly shut, not certain why she felt so warm, so protected, yet unwilling to investigate and risk putting an end to the delicious feeling of contentment that enveloped her.

She must be dreaming. Otherwise, why would her bed be rocking back and forth as though it traveled down an endless road, pulled by a team of speedy horses? And those rhythmic thumping sounds beneath her ear—had someone slipped a clock under her pillow? Stranger still, why would each breath she took make her think of Liam Whitcomb?

A pleasantly masculine aroma filled her senses, not unlike the faint, spicy scent of his shaving soap, and—

Emaline's eyes flew open. She gasped. No wonder she smelled Liam's soap—her face was pressed against his neckcloth! And that steady thumping in her ear was the beat of his heart. She was being held captive within the circle of his strong arms!

How had this happened? Even as she tried to make sense of the situation, she discovered that her own arms were beneath his coat, wound snugly around his waist. Embarrassment burned its way up her body as she realized she was as much captor as captive.

Aghast at this new development, Emaline remained perfectly still, trying to gather her wits. Unfortunately, she soon learned that astuteness was not easy to garner when one was locked in a gentleman's embrace. Especially when the rhythm of her heart seemed bent on matching itself to the beat of that life-sustaining organ in him, in much the same way her traitorous body had accommodated itself to the glorious hardness of his.

No. Do not think of such things!

After struggling to set her mind upon a less volatile path, she became aware of Liam's soft, steady breathing. Judging from the sound, he must be asleep. Grateful for that piece of good fortune, she endeavored to disentangle herself without waking him, for it would be much better all the way around if he knew nothing of this incident.

Moving slowly, she brought her left arm from behind his back and rested the palm of her hand on the seat for support while she freed her right. Unfortunately, her other arm was not so easy to extricate. It seemed to be caught between Liam's ribs and his forearm, almost as if he purposely held it fast.

Each time she tried to slip free, she felt his muscles ripple then bunch into solid bands of constraint. When she relaxed, so did those hard bands. Time and again she tried. Finally at the end of her patience, and not a little suspicious about those surging and relaxing muscles, she lifted her head to look into his face to see if he were truly asleep.

His eyes were closed, but to her dismay, his lips quivered. He was trying not to laugh!

Furious, Emaline used her free hand to give him a sound poke in the ribs. "Let me go, you unprincipled lout!"

Laughing aloud, Liam held her for only a few seconds more, then he let her go.

"How dare you?" she said, pushing away from him and putting as much distance between them as a closed chaise would allow.

"How dare *I?*" Laughter still close to the surface, he feigned innocence. "Fine talk, after you practically mauled me."

Emaline gasped. "I did no such thing!"

"I hesitate to contradict a lady, but you will notice, ma'am, that I am in *my* corner of the coach. I was napping—minding my own business, I might add—so you can imagine my surprise when I was suddenly roused from a deep slumber to find you in my corner as well." He concentrated upon the adjustment of his rumpled neckcloth. "I shall not even mention my astonishment when I felt you insinuating yourself against—"

"Insinuating!" Emaline grabbed up her discarded bonnet from the opposite seat, jerked it onto her head, and began to tie the sadly crushed ribbons beneath her chin.

"Actually," he amended, "insinuating might be a bit misleading."

"I should hope so. I—"

"It was more a sort of onslaught. The way you laid your head upon my chest, not to mention wrapping your arms around—"

"Sir! How shamelessly you—"

"Exactly what I thought myself," he interrupted pleasantly, ignoring her indignation. "Shameless is the very word. Call me old-fashioned if you will, but I consider it positively brazen for a single lady to thrust herself upon a gentleman in such a way."

Emaline stared at him in amazement. "Why, you—you know I never—"

"But then," he continued as though she had not spoken, "I remembered that technically you are a married woman, and as such, you mean to act with much more freedom than would be seemly in a lady not yet privy to the married state. Recalling that fact so put my mind at ease that I was able to ignore your unseemly conduct completely and resume my nap with a free conscience."

"Conscience! Sir, you have no conscience whatsoever. Not if you can relate such a whisker with a straight face."

Unable to maintain his composure a moment longer, Liam burst into laughter, a circumstance that put Emaline in sympathy with murderers the world over.

"I should warn you, Major, that I am at present enjoying a vision of you lying at my feet, a saber run through your black heart."

Not at all put off by such a confession, he merely bid her remember that she was a parson's daughter, then laughed again. Only when the door of the carriage was wrested open by the coachman did Liam see fit to beg her pardon for his rudeness.

Emaline vouchsafed no reply to his apology, however, for she realized with a start that they had arrived at Mrs. Zuber's.

She had been so engrossed in trying to show Liam how completely unmoved she was by his teasing that she had not even noticed the carriage coming to a stop. Nor had she attended to the earlier clack-clack of the horses' hooves upon the pavement. Similarly, until that moment she had been only minimally aware of the many vehicles moving about. Conveyances of all sort filled the city streets, from elegant carriages to dashing sporting vehicles, not to mention less noble hackneys and tradesmen's drays. With the coach stopped and the door opened, she was aware, as well, of the noise—subdued but still discernable—that spilled over into the residential area much like the hum of bees coming from a nearby hive.

"This be it, Maj—Your Lordship," the blue-coated postilion said, letting down the steps and moving aside. "Claymore Street, number twenty-one."

Emaline let Liam hand her out of the carriage for her first look at Mrs. Zuber's town house. She had not realized that London residences would be so tall, or so narrow. Four stories high and boasting scarcely twenty front feet, the edifice was a sturdy, yet dull brick, built flush with its neighbor on either side.

Standing on the sidewalk, Emaline looked straight up until she spied the twin chimneys at the roof line. Only when her bonnet threatened to fall off her tilted head did she remind herself not to act like a country miss, gawking for the edification of the passersby.

"Londoners must get most of their exercise from climbing stairs," she said.

"An unavoidable necessity," Liam replied. "With better than a million inhabitants, a city soon runs out of land and must utilize the sky."

While Emaline gazed her fill of the neat, if uninspiring neighborhood, the postilion came around to the side of the carriage, her trunk perched on his shoulder as though it weighed next to nothing. "Oh dear," she said, mindful of the fellow's back, "like those tall roofs, my head seems to be in the clouds. Let us delay no longer in apprising Mrs. Zuber of my arrival."

Hurrying up the four steps that gave onto a small stoop, Emaline reached her hand up to employ the knocker, only to discover that the item had been removed from the door. "What is this?" she asked, looking to Liam. "How is one expected to—" She stopped, not liking the worried expression on his face. "Have we come to the wrong place? Mrs. Zuber's is number twenty-one."

"The knocker is off the door," he said.

Emaline felt a sudden uneasiness. "And that signifies what, sir?"

Liam hesitated a moment before answering. "It indicates to would-be visitors that the family has gone out of town."

"But that cannot be."

For the first time since leaving the rectory, Emaline felt nervous, and very much alone. "Mrs. Zuber knew I was coming, for I wrote to her explaining my delay. Your man posted the letter right away, did he not?"

Without waiting for Liam's reply, she began beating upon the door with her fist. After a few minutes delay, the portal was opened by a female hardly more than a child, her mobcap and apron proclaiming her station within the house. "Yes, miss?" she said, bobbing a curtsey.

Reassured by the presence of the maid, Emaline said, "I am Miss Harrison, Mrs. Zuber's new companion. Be so good as to inform your employer that I have arrived, then kindly show the postilion where to take my trunk."

The servant's mouth fell open. "Lawks, miss. I can't!"

"You cannot what?" Liam asked, stepping forward.

The girl's eyes grew large as saucers in her thin face, and she looked as though she might soon burst into tears. "Beggin' your pardon, sir, but I can't do none of it. I can't tell

Mrs. Zuber on account of she be gone to Dorset to visit her daughter what's breeding, and I can't let miss in the house."

"Of course you can. Mrs. Zuber knew of Miss Harrison's delay. Surely she left instructions regarding her arrival."

"Instructions was left all right and tight, but they was for me not to let nobody in. 'Not nobody,' the mistress said, not if I valued my hide."

"You need have no concern for your skin," Emaline assured her, "for I will take full responsibility." She took a step forward as if to push past the maid, but the girl barred her way, holding fast to the door.

"The mistress give me a letter," she said, waiting until Emaline had stepped back before she relaxed her hold on the door. "Said I was to hand it to the new companion if she had the 'frontery to present herself."

Emaline swallowed a lump in her throat. Surely this was nothing more than a silly misunderstanding; something easily explained and rectified. Wishing she felt more confident in that assessment, she held out her hand. "Please give me the letter."

Reaching inside the pocket of her apron, the servant produced a single sheet of paper, folded and sealed with a blob of green wax. Once Emaline took the paper from her hand, the girl curtsied and shut the door, the finality of the resounding thud putting Emaline in mind of the gates of Heaven closing upon a sinner. Closing for all time.

Quickly, she tore open the seal and scanned the thin, stingy lines upon the page. At the end of the missive, she breathed deeply, hoping to steady her pounding heart. This could not be happening to her. She could not have come all the way to London only to be turned away upon her arrival. And her with only two guineas and a few copper coins until quarter day! Not even enough money to house her for the night and buy her a return ticket to Bartholsby.

Not wanting to believe the evidence of her eyes, she read through the letter a second time, taking care not to skip even one angry word. When she finished, she folded the paper neatly and put it inside her reticule.

"I am dismissed," she said quietly. "Mrs. Zuber dislikes being kept waiting."

Chapter 5

Liam cursed beneath his breath. "The old witch!"

This observation having covered both their opinions upon Mrs. Zuber's character, they stood quietly for several moments, neither of them wishing to be the first to voice the question of what was to be done now. It was the postilion who finally broke the silence.

"What you want I should do with her ladyship's trunk, sir?"

"Return it to the boot," Liam replied. Then taking Emaline's arm, he opened the carriage door and helped her back inside. She went without demur.

"Have you any friends to whom you could go?" he asked once they were seated and the rattle of the coach's wheels was heard upon the cobblestones.

"Not in London. Nor," she continued, embarrassment softening her voice almost to a whisper, "have I money enough with me to pay for a night's lodging at a hotel."

"It is of no consequence," he said, not unkindly. "Had you a million pounds, I fear it would not buy you lodging at any of London's respectable hotels. You are a woman alone. No concierge worth his salt would extend the courtesy of the house to a lady traveling without so much as an abigail."

This pronouncement being unanswerable, Emaline said nothing.

After a silence that lasted only a few moments, but that felt to Emaline like hours, Liam snapped his fingers as if recalling something. Letting down the glass at the windows he called up to his coachman.

"Yes, m'lord?"

"Grosvenor Square," he called. "Number seventeen Brook Street."

When the glass was once again in place and Liam had resumed his seat, Emaline asked rather timidly whose house was at seventeen Brook Street.

"Yours," he answered.

Thinking perhaps she had misheard him, Emaline said, "I beg your pardon."

"Yours for the moment, in any case. It was my cousin's town house, and unless someone comes forward to contest his will, it is yours until you choose to dispose of it."

"But I—"

He waved aside her words as though he knew what she was about to say. "I am fully aware of your feelings regarding the will, but I perceive this to be an emergency. So I pray you, spare me both your ethical objections and your metaphysical philosophies upon the subject."

"I will offer you neither," she answered meekly, "for I am prodigiously grateful not to be obliged to spend the evening loitering about the streets with only the stars for a roof."

Although it wanted a good hour before the stars appeared, dusk was gathering by the time Liam's coachman pulled up before Lord Seymour's town house in Grosvenor Square. Even so, there was yet enough light for Emaline to discern the subtle differences between the streets and houses of Mayfair and those of Mrs. Zuber's neighborhood. Though her would-be employer lived on a respectable street just north of Russell Square, it enjoyed neither the quiet nor the exclusivity of the squares of Mayfair—that section of town where in the previous century a rowdy cattle and general fair was held each May, but where the cream of London society now chose to live.

The tall brick residences of Grosvenor Square were slightly wider than those of Claymore Street, and while they maintained the architectural simplicity that epitomized the facades of Claymore, the Grosvenor Square homes boasted a number of decorative elements that set them apart. Seymour House had an intricately wrought fanlight, while the ground-floor windows featured both pediments and arched tops.

In addition, number seventeen Brook Street displayed an item that distinguished it from its neighbors—attached to the door knocker was a black crepe wreath.

As Liam assisted her from the carriage, he noticed the wreath. "I see the news of your husband's demise has reached town before us. Good. That is one less obstacle we shall be obliged to confront."

Without further ado he took the steps two at a time and sounded the knocker. The summons was answered promptly by a tall, middle-aged butler dressed in a blue coat of modern cut. Vastly different from the aged butler at Seymour Park, the servant bowed with the punctiliousness of a duke, then stepped aside to permit the lady and gentleman to enter the vestibule.

"I am George Turner," he said. "Permit me to welcome you to Seymour House, my lord."

Stepping forward, Liam allowed the man to take his hat and gloves. "You know me, then?"

"Yes, sir. You have a look of your father. A fine man was Mr. Whitcomb, if I may be so bold."

"Thank you, Turner."

Liam motioned toward the black crepe. "I see you were informed of his lordship's death."

"Yes, my lord. We were notified by mail of the accident and its unfortunate consequence by Mr. Chapham, Lord Sey—that is to say, the late Lord Seymour's solicitor."

The *we* to whom the butler referred was explained by the sound of soft footsteps. From somewhere in the rear of the house, two females came forward, stopping near the bottom of the narrow, unpretentious staircase that led to the upper floors. One of the women, plump and in her late thirties, was dressed in the black bombazine and frilled cap of a housekeeper; the other, a comely, blond girl of about twenty, wore the apron and mobcap of a housemaid.

"Mrs. Turner," the butler said, indicating the housekeeper, "and Hannah Rice."

Both women bobbed curtseys.

"In the solicitor's letter," Liam asked, "did he inform you that this house was left to *Lady* Seymour?"

"He did, sir."

Not by so much as a raised eyebrow did the very superior servant betray his personal opinion of deathbed brides or of widows who chose to travel abroad without the least sign of their bereavement upon their person. "On the chance that her ladyship might choose to pay us a visit soon, we have done what we could to make the master bedchamber agreeable to a lady."

Taking Emaline's unintelligible murmur as both thanks and introduction, he bowed once again. "Shall I have Mrs. Turner show you upstairs, my lady?"

"Yes, please."

As the housekeeper came forward and curtsied, Emaline turned to give her hand to Liam. "Thank you, Lord Seymour, for escorting me. If we should not meet again, I—"

"We shall meet tomorrow afternoon," he informed her. "I will call upon you, if for no other reason than to assure myself that you survived your first night in town. Tonight I must return to my home in Surrey, for I have promised to escort my sister and her chaperone to town on the morrow. If you should wish it, I will bring back with me a list of solicitors from which you may choose a man to handle your affairs."

"But I cannot stay in London!"

"You can and you must stay."

"How can I, now that Mrs. Zuber has—" Emaline caught herself just in time. She wanted no one else privy to her embarrassing dismissal from her post as paid companion. "You, of all people, must see the wisdom of my returning to Bartholsby."

In a more conciliatory tone, Liam said, "Please stay. If only for a few days. Just until this business of the will is settled. I am persuaded the Turners will know how to make you comfortable."

"We shall do our best, my lord," the butler added.

"But I—"

"Furthermore," Liam continued, interrupting her protest, "I cannot believe you would wish to return to Wiltshire before seeing at least a few of the historical landmarks of the city."

In this Liam had guessed correctly. Noting a spark of interest in her tired face, he smiled. "In addition to the list of solicitors," he said, "I shall also bring you a guidebook."

For the moment, Emaline was too exhausted to think of a logical reason for refusing his offer. Too much had happened to her in the past three days. She needed time to assimilate it all. Her removal from her childhood home, her sudden marriage and widowhood, her trip to town, and then the shock of being fired from the job she had depended upon to supply her with both a home and respectable chaperonage while in London—the seriousness of these events had finally combined to take their toll upon her strength. She felt ready to drop where she stood.

With a brief nod of assent, Emaline replied, "It shall be as you wish, sir. I will remain for a few days."

Liam raised her fingertips almost to his lips, bid her a restful night, then watched as she followed the housekeeper up the stairs. When she was out of sight, he retrieved his hat and gloves from the butler and placed a small stack of guineas in the servant's hand. "See that her ladyship has everything she needs, beginning with a light repast in her room before she retires."

"Yes, my lord." The butler slipped the gold coins inside his coat without looking at them, but a decided thaw had begun in his frosty manner.

"And when I return tomorrow, Turner, if you will have a Dutch reckoning of the outstanding household bills, I will place it in the capable hands of my man of business. I would not wish Lady Seymour to be disturbed by any overzealous tradesmen seeking recompense for my cousin's debts."

A smile very nearly broke through the butler's dignified demeanor. "It shall be as you wish, my lord."

It was at least two hours later when Liam entered the bookroom at Whitcomb Hall. Owing to the full moon, the fifteen-mile drive from town had not been difficult, but after being on the road for the better part of the day, he was happy to be home where he need face no further crises.

Unfortunately, he was not in the house above a half dozen minutes before he was disabused of that rose-colored assumption. After having requested the footman to find him a plate of sandwiches and a tankard of something—anything—he had removed from the inside pocket of his coat the jeweler's box Emaline had given him the day before. He had only just begun to study the necklace—a necklace whose exact double resided in the safe in this very room—when someone knocked upon the door and entered the room.

"Major," began his valet without preamble, "you've come 'ome in good time, you 'ave, for it's a rare tempest in a teacup we've got 'ere. And the ladies will not listen to reason."

Liam swore, a circumstance that caused Felix Harvey to relax. The short, wiry servant, Liam's batman all through the war years, was much better able to deal with gentlemen and their tempers—vile language included—than with the bouts of tears employed by the fair sex.

"What's amiss?" Liam asked, returning the box to his pocket, then disposing himself in one of the red leather wing chairs, stretching his long, muscular legs out before him. "Can a man not set both feet in the house before chaos descends upon him?"

"Exactly what I thought meself, sir." Without waiting for permission, the valet perched upon the edge of the desk, ready to inform his employer of the goings-on in the house.

Liam took no offense at his valet's presumption in seating himself, for Felix Harvey was both less and more than a true gentleman's gentleman. It was to the homely batman, with his sparse brown hair and his sharp gray eyes that Liam owed his very life.

Were it not for the resourceful Harvey—a product of the London slums—Liam would now be residing in a French graveyard. Not content with removing the wounded major from the carnage of the Toulouse battlefield, the little man had carried the larger upon his back for several miles before he found a doctor he could threaten or bribe into removing the bullet and binding up Liam's wounds. And it was Harvey who had nursed him through the feverish days when his life hung so precariously in the balance between this world and the next.

The debt too large to repay, Liam had offered him *carte blanche*—a home, a business, a pension for life—he need only name his wishes, but the proud and independent batman had wanted nothing more than to continue in the major's employ.

"I 'ad no more than reached the 'ouse," he said, bringing Liam's thoughts back to the new crisis, "and was on me way to me room to unpack me traps, when Miss Cordia sends 'er maid to fetch me. Fair red-eyed she was from crying, and—"

"My sister?" Liam sat up, his fatigue forgotten. "Has something happened to Cordia?"

"Not to 'er. It's Mrs. Persimmon-Face what's laid abed. Broke 'er leg she 'as. 'Er *limb,* she calls it, like as if the Almighty made 'er a tree instead of a two-legged creature like the rest of us."

Warming to a popular theme, he continued, "Not that it wasn't just like the old block of wood to go and ruin a person's fun. 'Ow like 'er to break a leg the day before she was to take miss to town to purchase 'er come-out *fol-lols.* Miss Cordia's 'eart is fair broke, Major, and that's a fact."

THE RUBY NECKLACE 83

Liam had only just assimilated this news of the chaperone's misfortune when the door swung open and a blur of yellow-sprigged muslin burst into the room and ran to him. "Liam," cried his sister, her voice quivery, "has Harvey told you of Mrs. Pruett? That she—she—"

Like a dutiful brother, Liam allowed his sister to throw herself into his arms. Deciding his coat and neckcloth were as good as ruined forever, he gathered the young lady close—much as he had gathered Emaline earlier—and let her have her moment of tears. When the lachrymose outpouring was finally stanched, however, he bid her take the seat opposite his and tell him the whole.

"For I can do nothing to repair the damage, Cordia, until I know the extent of your chaperone's injuries. Is Mrs. Pruett's leg truly broken, or has she merely sustained a sprain?"

Miss Cordia Whitcomb took the chair her brother indicated. Dabbing at her pretty nose with a minuscule piece of white lawn and lace, she gave her brother a brief version of the accident and its results.

"It is not a sprain," she said. "Somehow Mrs. Pruett missed the bottom stair, and as she fell, she suffered a broken shinbone. Doctor Vinson encased her leg in a plaster, dosed her with laudanum, and put her to bed . . . where he says she must stay for at least a fortnight."

"Humph," the valet muttered. "There be no *must* about it. Mrs. Prune-Puss will *choose* to stay in that bed for the next twenty years, or me name ain't Felix 'Arvey! If you was to ask me, she's invented a nice cushy retirement scheme for 'erself. Jumped at the main chance, she 'as. No more 'iring 'erself out to show young misses the ropes. No more racketing about town till all hours of the night. The way I see it, Major, at 'er time of life, she's fair got tired, she 'as, and—"

This impassioned reading of the hired companion's character was interrupted by the arrival of the footman with a tray of sandwiches and a tankard of beer. A respite greeted with enthusiasm by Liam.

After setting the tray on the small drum table close to Liam's chair, the servant asked, "Will that be all, m'lord?"

"My lord," his sister echoed. "How strange to hear you referred to in that manner." Then, as though recalling the subject uppermost in her own mind, she said, "When I got your letter informing me of Cousin Ambrose's death, Mrs. Pruett said we must delay my come-out until after a proper mourning period had been observed. An entire three months!" The young lady looked at her brother, appeal in her eyes. "Must we?"

Liam took a deep swallow from the tankard before answering. "We will not mourn. Not for even one day. Ambrose Whitcomb was a miserable excuse for a man, and not content with repaying our father's many kindnesses with continued animosity, he tried what he could to ruin our lives. Why should we honor a man who showed our father nothing but disrespect?"

Miss Cordia stared, surprised by this answer. "But what will people—"

"In this instance," he replied, "the world may say what it wishes. Lady Seymour refused to play the hypocrite, and I have chosen to follow her lead."

"Lady Seymour?" Cordia's soft blue eyes were round with surprise. "But I thought Cousin Ambrose was a widower."

Liam cursed himself for letting that particular cat escape the bag. "He married again just prior to his death."

Miss Cordia's mouth fell open. "But who would marry such a man? And why?"

Not wishing to reveal the true nature of the marriage, Liam delayed his answer by the simple expedient of lifting the tankard to his lips. While he sipped slowly of the brew, his sister continued to speak.

"Of course," she remarked with all the wisdom of her eighteen years, "I do not suppose older ladies are all that particular about who they wed."

Liam very nearly choked on his beer, and while he coughed, Felix Harvey took it upon himself to enlighten the young lady. " 'Er ladyship ain't so old as all that."

"Really? Is she youngish, then?"

Recovered from his bout of coughing, Liam replied, "Age—like beauty—is in the eye of the beholder." Noting his sister's dissatisfaction at such a nebulous answer, he added, "Lady Seymour is a few years younger than me."

"Younger than you! And married to a man older than our father." She wrinkled her nose. "How disgusting. I am sure I wish her happy of her bargain."

"You will mend your tone, if you please," instructed her brother. "Emaline is a lady in every sense of the word, and we will show her proper respect."

Cordia stared, more intrigued than offended by his sharp tone. "Emaline, did you say?" When she received no answer, she said, "Such a pretty name. Do you not agree?"

Liam took another sip from the tankard.

She waited until he had swallowed and set the tankard aside. "Shall I like her?"

"Who can say?"

"What of you, then? Do you like her?"

Liam considered the question a moment, remembering the way Emaline had felt in his arms . . . the way he had felt when he held her. "She makes me laugh."

Noting the speculative look in his sister's eye, and wishing to forestall any further discussion of their new relative, he steered the topic back to the chaperone. "As to the subject of your come-out, our cousin's demise will necessitate no postponement. However, if Mrs. Pruett is unable to fulfill her duties as chaperone, I fear you will be obliged to wait until spring."

"But, I—" The young lady lowered her head until her small pointed chin very nearly touched her chest. The thick, dusky curls that were held back by a satin ribbon fell forward, hiding from her brother's view both her profile and her disappointment.

"I am genuinely sorry, my dear, for I know how much you have been looking forward to the little season."

Lifting her face, she looked at him, her lower lip caught between her teeth to still its trembling. "You have no need to apologize. No brother could have been more generous. Or more patient. Only . . ."

"Only?" he repeated quietly.

"It is just that spring seems so far away. Is there no hope at all for a new chaperone?"

Liam shook his head. "I fear not. Surely you remember what a difficult time I had convincing Mrs. Pruett to bring you out."

Felix Harvey saw fit to add his tuppence worth. "Fair 'ad to beg the old vinegar-puss, the major did. Not to mention doling out an 'efty sum to get 'er to agree. Acted like she was Queen Charlotte 'erself, bestowing favors on the masses."

The young lady's voice was a mere whisper. "Was she terribly expensive?"

Liam cast the valet a quelling look before returning his attention to his sister. "The cost is of no importance. What is relevant here is that professional chaperones, at least the ones who are acceptable to the *ton,* are snapped up quite early. And for that reason, I cannot believe we would be able to find another within days of the beginning of the little season."

A poignant sigh was the young lady's only reply.

"Buck up, lass," Felix Harvey advised. "You 'ave but eighteen summers in your dish. Another six months more or less won't matter so very much in the grand scheme of things."

It was not to be wondered at that this piece of advice failed dismally as a rallier of flagging spirits, and as Cordia walked slowly to the door, her shoulders sagged in dejection. Just as she stretched her hand toward the doorknob, however, she paused, standing stock-still, as though held in check by some unseen force.

"I have it!" she said. Her shoulders squared as if by magic, and when she turned back to look at her brother, the pretty face that had been so sad only moments earlier was now made beautiful by a glorious smile.

"Liam! I know who we can ask to be my chaperone. In fact, I am amazed that you did not think of her yourself, for she is the very person."

The two men stared at each other, neither of them able to guess who 'the very person' might be.

"I shall ask my cousin to chaperone me," Cordia informed them happily. "I shall ask Lady Seymour."

Chapter 6

Blithely unaware that she figured once again as the one person most suitable to save the Whitcomb family from disaster, Emaline stretched lazily, enjoying the comfort of the massive ebony bed. Well rested, she sat up, stacked the pillows behind her back, then surveyed with interest the master suite of the Seymour town house.

The morning sunlight streaming through the four floor-to-ceiling windows in the adjacent dressing room gave her a better view of the furnishings than had been possible by last evening's candlelight. The larger of the two rooms on the second floor, the rear bedchamber had been carefully divested of whatever masculine accoutrements had been left there by Lord Ambrose Seymour. Now the handsome old washstand with its Staffordshire blue and white cistern held a cup containing Emaline's tooth powder and brush, while upon the polished top of the Chippendale Beau Brummel, with its stand-up looking glass, reposed her silver comb and brush set, a gift from her father on the occasion of her eighteenth birthday.

In a further attempt to make the room appear to be hers, someone had draped Emaline's plain lawn dressing gown across the high back of a barber's chair that stood in the corner nearest the empty fireplace. As well, they had placed in the padded seat of the chair the little book she had inadvertently failed to return to the vitrine at Seymour Park. Blushing that she had been caught again with the scandalous missive in her possession, she hoped that whoever had been thoughtful enough to put it there had not read the title.

Contrary to her fears that the servants would feel she was an interloper, her reception had been more than gracious. The Turners and Hannah had outdone themselves in an attempt to make her feel at home. And though she still considered herself a guest in the town house, she appreciated the effort taken on her behalf.

Mrs. Turner had practically begged her to allow them to fill the hip bath in the dressing room, insisting it was no trouble at all, and declaring that a hot soak was just what Emaline needed to loosen all those parts of the anatomy that stiffened on a long journey. When Emaline finally agreed, they brought enough hot water to allow her to soak for half an hour, time enough to loosen the most recalcitrant of muscles.

After her bath, she discovered that her pampering was not yet finished, for a light repast awaited her convenience. Feeling positively decadent, she ate while tucked up in the large bed—a thing she had never done before without the excuse of some childhood illness. Hungry, she devoured every spoonful of the delicious consommé and every morsel of the two hot, flaky scones served with the housekeeper's own orange marmalade.

Clean, comfortable, and well fed, Emaline had soon fallen into a deep, restful sleep. Someone must have come and removed the dishes, for they were no longer in evidence, yet the new Lady Seymour had heard nothing, sleeping through the night and waking refreshed and eager to start a new day.

Leaning back against the pillows, she went over the plans she had made while luxuriating in the bath the night before. At first she had been too shocked by the loss of her position as Mrs. Zuber's companion to think clearly, but once she relaxed she remembered that she was not without an advisor in London. Mr. Fenster Wooten, the solicitor who administered the trust left her by her grandfather, had offices near Lincoln's Inn.

She would turn over to Mr. Wooten the matter of settling Lord Ambrose Seymour's will, while at the same time procuring from the solicitor an advance upon that portion of the sixty pounds per annum due her on the next quarter day. And if she had any money left in her reticule after arranging her return to Bartholsby, she meant to see a bit of London. She might not be able to fulfill her wish to experience the world—there was no time for visiting the theaters and the museums—but she could see a few of the wondrous buildings. Perhaps a stroll through the park or even a visit to one or two of the shops might be possible.

Pleased with her plans, she was happy to hear a soft rap upon her door. "Come in," she called.

"Good morning, m'lady."

"Good morning, Hannah. Is that chocolate I smell?"

"It is, ma'am."

Setting the small tray on the bedside table, the maid poured the steaming liquid from the blue-patterned pot into a matching china cup, then handed the cup to Emaline. "Mrs. Turner wants I should ask if you desire to have your breakfast brought to your room."

Emaline shook her head. "Thank her for me, but this chocolate will suffice until I return from my errand."

"Your errand, m'lady?" As she spoke, the maid went into the dressing room, opened the clothespress, and began laying out such undergarments as she deemed necessary for her new mistress's morning toilette. "Do you wish to visit the shops, your ladyship?"

"No. I wish to visit the offices of Messrs. Wooten and Jova, for I must speak with my solicitor as soon as possible. Do you suppose Turner can direct me to Lincoln's Inn? That is somewhere in the City, I believe."

The maid's raised eyebrows revealed her surprise at such a question. "Mr. Turner knows the City like it was his own village, ma'am, but I'm certain he would say he ought to send a message round to the solicitor requesting the gentleman call upon you here at Seymour House."

"But there is no need to send for Mr. Wooten. I am perfectly able to go to his office." Emaline sipped the warm liquid, closing her eyes in enjoyment of the aromatic brew. "As a matter of fact, I look forward to the drive. I wish to see a little of the town, and this may be my only opportunity. Once I go home to Wiltshire, I shall probably never return to London."

To Emaline's surprise, this quite innocent remark brought about a rapid change in the maid's demeanor. Her mouth began to tremble, while tears filled her pretty eyes. "Never return, m'lady? But we thought—we had hoped . . ." A sob caught in the girl's throat.

Horrified, Emaline put the half-filled cup on the bed table, tossed the covers aside, then hurried to the dressing room where she took the girl's work-roughened hands in hers. "My dear, whatever have I said to make you weep?"

"Please," she said, kneeling before Emaline, "don't go."

"But, I—"

"If you leave, the house'll be closed up. Then what is to

become of me and the Turners? We'll be turned off, we will. And with no place to go. Things been hard enough for us these past two years, but leastwise we had a roof over our heads and summit in our bellies."

Emaline was unprepared for this impassioned plea. "There is no need for this display, I assure you, for your employment does not depend upon me or my comings and goings."

The moment she uttered the words, Emaline wondered if they were less than the truth. If the will were contested, and as a result wound up in either Consistory or Prerogative Court, it could be tied up for years. The unbelievable delays in Chancery suits were a common subject for cartoons and broadsides. If the will became lost in the court system, the house might, indeed, be closed up and the servants dismissed.

Not wishing to add to the maid's distress, Emaline kept her thoughts to herself. "Dry your eyes, Hannah, there's a good girl."

The maid did as she was bid, making use of the hem of her apron to wipe away the tears. "Beggin' your pardon, m'lady," she said between sniffs.

"Think nothing of it," Emaline replied. Naturally, she did not take her own advice, for the girl's anguish reminded her of her own helpless feeling last evening when she discovered that Mrs. Zuber had given her the sack. Of course, in her case, Emaline had a modest trust fund to fall back on. She might be inconvenienced, but she would never be destitute.

"You speak of no place to go, Hannah. Did you put none of your salary away to sustain you in the event of an emergency?"

Hannah shook her head. "There ain't been no money to put by."

"Impossible," Emaline said. "Lord Seymour was often at the town house, and though he cared not one whit to whom he owed money, or if the accounts were ever paid, his man of business saw to it that the servants always received their money. Mr. Chapham informed me of that fact, and though I did not care for the man, I cannot believe he told me a falsehood. According to him, even when his lordship stayed in the country, the town staff received board wages."

The girl nodded, her mobcap nearly toppling off her thick blond curls. "Mr. Chapham told it right, m'lady. I got my two pounds, ten shillings each quarter. Even when the greengrocer and the collier were hammering on the door demanding their bills be paid, the Turners and me got ours. Only every time the wages came, there was Mr. Brofton, smiling his weasel's smile, his hand out ready to take the money from us."

"Brofton? Do you mean Ambrose's valet?"

The girl's shudder was her answer.

"What gives Vernon Brofton the right to take your money?"

Hannah shrugged her shoulders. "Don't nobody give him the right, m'lady. He just takes it."

"And no one tries to stop him?"

"Once Mr. Turner stood up to him. Said he was through paying. Said Brofton had been robbing them for years, and they wasn't sitting still for it no more."

"Good for Turner!"

"No, ma'am. It weren't good. Far from it. Mr. Brofton just cursed him for his troubles, then dealt him a vicious doubler. Mr. Turner weren't expecting it, and he crumpled over and fell to the floor. And while the poor man lay there moaning with pain, the valet jumped on him, hitting him with facer after facer, rendering him near senseless. 'You owe me,' Brofton yelled after each blow. 'You owe me.' "

It was Emaline's turn to shudder. "Poor Turner. A bad thing, indeed, to be in debt to an animal like Brofton. Have you any idea why he owes the man?"

"No, ma'am. Though I overheard Mrs. Turner crying later, while I was scrubbing the blood off the kitchen floor. Between sobs, she was wailing something about how this was all Samuel's fault."

Emaline felt as if she was getting in over her head. "And who is Samuel?"

"Near as I can figure, he's Mr. Turner's brother."

"You do not know him, then?"

"No, m'lady. Never laid eyes on him. And not likely to, neither, for I think he's doing hard labor."

Emaline gasped. "A convict? Are you certain?"

"Certain as I can be without being told straight out. When I overheard Mrs. Turner, she was saying something about how gathering ballast for shipping on the Thames was too good for the likes of Samuel Turner. 'He ought to have been deported,' she said."

So, Emaline thought, Turner's brother was a criminal, and Vernon Brofton knew it and was augmenting his valet's salary with a little blackmailing. Not that the Turners could be held accountable for unlawful acts committed by someone else, even a relative. Still, it might lose them their jobs if the connection became public knowledge. Of course, Brofton had claimed that *George* Turner owed him.

Strange.

Recollecting that Hannah was being extorted as well, Emaline said, "I still do not understand why the valet is taking your money."

"Lots of reasons, m'lady. Could be because I saw him beat up Mr. Turner. Or perhaps it's his way of paying me back for refusing him every time he invited me to go to the pub. He's a bully, and bullies don't need a reason for their meanness. He takes my gelt just to show me he can."

This being unanswerable, Emaline kept her thoughts to herself. While the maid helped her dress, however, she made a silent vow to inform Liam of the extortion. As a wealthy and powerful man, he was in a position to do something about it. She was not.

Surprisingly, she felt no hesitancy about asking Liam for help. She knew she could trust him to put a stop to the terrorizing of the three servants. If she was certain of anything, it was her total conviction that Liam would not refuse her request.

Mr. Fenster Wooten, on the other hand, had no difficulty whatever in refusing Emaline's request for an early payment of her trust fund money. When she visited the wiry little solicitor, whose hair spiked out like a porcupine's and whose personality matched his hair, he flatly rejected her petition. Although he agreed to look into the matter of Lord Seymour's will, he refused to advance so much as a shilling from the trust.

"Be more cautious in the future," he advised. "Sir Gerald stipulated that you should be paid each quarter day, and I see no reason to go against his instructions."

"But my grandfather would not have wished me to be destitute."

"Destitute? What nonsense. Mere female hysteria. I advise you to return to Grosvenor Square. Remain there. Your being in residence can only strengthen your case as beneficiary."

"But I do not wish to remain there!"

When no amount of argument swayed the little man's resolve to abide by the terms of the trust, Emaline was forced to return to Seymour House. As the hackney tooled westward on Oxford Street, she refused to look about her at the sights she had found so enjoyable on the earlier trip. Blinded by her fury at the high-handedness of the pompous solicitor, she was in no mood for gawking at the buildings they drove past.

How could she remain at Seymour House until quarter day? That was four weeks away. She could not do it! And yet, with two pounds in her reticule, how could she do anything else?

She still had not arrived at a satisfactory solution to the dilemma of what to do when the hackney turned onto Brook Street. As they pulled up to the curb at number seventeen, she saw that another carriage was there before them. A groom in tasteful blue livery stood at the heads of a pair of perfectly matched grays that were hitched to a handsome maroon curricle.

The owner of the curricle was not in evidence, but Emaline had no difficulty in guessing the visitor's identity. Liam had said he would call today, and he was a man of his word.

In fact, the gentleman had been shown to what passed for a drawing room some twenty minutes earlier, and he rose with obvious relief when Emaline arrived.

"Lady Seymour," he said politely, taking her hand and lifting it almost to his lips. "I hope your meeting with your solicitor was fruitful."

Not wishing to reveal the outcome of the interview, she chose not to answer his remark, looking about her instead at the dark, cluttered, and very dreary room. "And I hope, sir, that you will not have fallen into a fit of the dismals while waiting in this mausoleum. Why did no one open the drapery to let in the light?"

"Possibly," he answered affably, "because there are no windows."

Until this moment, Emaline had been in only the master bedroom and the vestibule. And though Hannah had described the layout of the house, nothing had prepared her for the reality of this chamber, where candlelight cast eerie shadows upon the dark walls.

As the house was originally built, the dining room was situated at the front of the house, facing the street, while this room was at the rear, looking onto the small garden. When the dressing room was added abovestairs, a corresponding room was added off the back of the ground floor, trapping the drawing room in the middle and leaving it windowless.

The addition had been meant as a gentleman's library, but over the years, with no hostess in the house, the masculine decor had spilled over into the drawing room. Now the chamber was barely recognizable as a place where ladies might wish to congregate. Or anyone else, Emaline decided.

Bidding Liam be seated in one of the dark leather chairs that flanked the empty fireplace, she opened the pocket doors, entered the library, and walked around to the far side of the kneehole desk, where thick red damask drapes covered the windows. After finding the center opening, she pushed the heavy material aside as far as possible, letting in the early-afternoon sunlight. The double sets of French windows, she discovered, were sealed tight and could not be opened to admit the fresh air, but at least the light dispelled some of the cheerless atmosphere.

"Whew," she remarked, returning to Liam, who had remained standing. "How could anyone endure such a dark room?" Smiling mischievously, she said, "I begin to wonder, sir, if your relative was a vampire."

The corners of Liam's mouth twitched. "As my cousin's wife, madam, you would know his nocturnal habits better than I."

"You know I nev—" Pausing in the midst of her instinctive denial, she spied the teasing light in those dark blue eyes. "Touché," she said, conceding the point.

Liam bowed in acknowledgement of her sportsmanship. "If the room displeases you, ma'am, let us leave it by all means. Might I suggest a drive? My curricle is at your disposal."

Deciding she could speak more freely where there was no risk of being overheard, she agreed to his suggestion. "I should like to go for a drive, sir. Will you allow me a few minutes to change my hat? If I am to ride in an open carriage, I shall need a bonnet with a wider poke."

Liam was pleased to note that she was true to her word, reappearing quite promptly. Over her fern-green frock she had added a spencer of pomona green faille. Completing the outfit was a Coburg bonnet whose high crown was adorned with dark ivy leaves and whose wide poke was trimmed with pomona green ribbons. From beneath the tied ribbons peeped provocative wisps of coppery hair.

He looked her over with pleasure. Though the ensemble was not in the first style of elegance, it was becoming to her coloring, while its simple lines complimented her trim figure. Offering her his arm, he led her out to his curricle, admitting, if only to himself, that a man would have no cause to avoid the main thoroughfares with Emaline on the box beside him.

As for the lady, she found the gentleman's ocher brown

coat completely to her liking, reinforcing the rather fanciful impression she had of him as a man of the elements—earth, and sky, and sun. Nor had she failed to notice the way both the coat and his buff-colored trousers fit to perfection his long, lean physique, subtly accenting the symmetry and shape of his muscles.

She approved as well of the way he placed his beaver hat at a jaunty angle upon his dark blond hair just prior to handing her into the carriage.

"You may wait for me here," he told the groom.

"Yes, m'lord."

Once his master had the ribbons in hand, the servant stepped away from the horses' heads.

Not until the curricle had left the boundaries of Grosvenor Square well behind and was approaching Mount Street did Liam speak to his companion. "Shall I turn them to the right and head for the park? Or is there some other sight you particularly wished to see?"

"Westminster Abbey," she answered without hesitation.

Liam smiled. "Ever a decisive lady," he said, guiding the team to the left.

"You asked my preference," she reminded him.

"And I did so because I wished to know it. I was merely remembering aloud that you are a lady who knows her own mind."

"Similarly, I am remembering aloud that decisiveness in females is not a trait most gentlemen look upon with favor."

"I cannot speak for most gentlemen. Only for myself."

"And speaking for yourself, do you object to females who think for themselves?"

"In my experience, far too many people follow the trends of the times, relinquishing their own convictions for whatever standards are in fashion at the moment. I admire strength of character, no matter in which of the sexes I find it."

Emaline looked to see if he was in earnest. Since he gave his attention to the handling of his team, however, she could not see his face. Unable to read anything from his strong profile, she asked. "And what if that person of character holds an opinion that differs from your own, sir? Would your admiration prove constant?"

He cast her an amused glance. "Certainly not! A person of discernment would, quite naturally, agree with every word I utter. If she did not, I should be obliged to reconsider my judgment of her character and relabel it not strength, but wrong-headedness."

Emaline found it impossible not to respond to this absurdity. A chuckle escaped her lips. "Sir! You are making sport of me."

"Madam," he replied, "I could not resist."

For her part, she found it difficult to resist that slow, half-smile that crinkled the corners of his mouth. "I begin to suspect that you are an unreclaimable tease."

The smile disappeared, and just a hint of regret crept into his voice. "I am reclaimed now. Thanks primarily to Emperor Napoleon and his wish to rule the world no matter how great the cost. However, jesting was once my besetting sin."

"Once?"

His answering remark, whatever it was, was eclipsed by a sudden and rather acrimonious meeting of a pair of drays, the one driver wishing to turn northwest off Shaftesbury, the other bearing in that same direction off Piccadilly, and neither willing to surrender the right of way. Only Liam's quick reactions and his able handling of the team kept the curricle from crashing into the deadlocked carts just ahead. With a swiftness that took Emaline's breath away, he deftly guided the horses around the impasse, the left wheel of the curricle missing that of the dray by mere inches.

"Are you all right?" he asked, once they were out of harm's way.

"I believe so," she replied, relaxing her death grip on his arm and hoping fervently that he would fail to notice the mauling she had given the sleeve of his elegant coat. "But if London traffic is always this hectic, I marvel that the streets are not strewn with bodies from one end of town to the other."

The image of hapless pedestrians knocked down while attempting to cross the road put Emaline in mind of Vernon Brofton and his vicious attack upon the butler. Now might be as good a time as any to relate the story to Liam.

Before she could broach the subject, however, her companion initiated a quite different conversation. "Your mentioning strewn bodies puts me in mind of something my sister wished me to discuss with you."

His voice had an odd quality to it, almost as if having introduced the topic, he wished he could unsay it. Yet when she turned to look at him, the only indication of his reluctance was the rather resolute set of his square jaw.

"Your sister wished you to speak with me about strewn bodies?"

"Fallen, actually. And in the singular."

"I do not follow you, sir."

As though wishing to get over rough ground as lightly as possible, Liam hurriedly explained the hired chaperone's unfortunate misstep, the resulting broken leg, and his sister's disappointment at having to postpone her come-out.

"My sympathies to both ladies," Emaline said politely.

"Though to tell the truth, I fail to see why Miss Whitcomb wished me to know of the accident. Did she think I might be acquainted with someone who would be a suitable replacement for the injured chaperone?"

"In a manner of speaking."

Once again, Emaline heard that odd, reluctant quality in his voice, and something about it put her in mind of the night he talked—nay, maneuvered—her into marrying his cousin.

Warning bells sounded in her head. The man was not above using her for his family's benefit; he had proven that once already. Suddenly suspicious, she turned to stare at him. Surely he would not have the nerve to ask her to serve as chaperone to his sister. It would be tantamount to an insult, for she was seven and twenty, not seven and forty. And though well past her first blush of youth, she considered herself far too young to be a chaperone!

He turned his face slightly toward her, and in those dark blue eyes there was a look that was part apology, part amusement, and part pure audacity.

He did have the nerve!

Emaline balled her hands into fists. "Allow me to inform you, Liam Whitcomb, that you have the world's own gall!"

Chapter 7

"No! I cannot do it. And what is more, I will not do it."

"Of course not," Liam answered quietly. "It was a totally preposterous notion. For one thing, anyone can see that you are much too young to be a chaperone."

Although Emaline had been thinking that exact same thing only seconds before, his saying it had a placating effect upon her, cooling her original anger. "Believe me, my sympathies are with Miss Whitcomb, for I know she must be heartbroken, but I would be totally unsuitable as a chaperone for a young lady wishing to enter society. To be properly introduced, she needs the sponsorship of a matron who possesses at least a few important connections. I have none whatsoever. Furthermore, I have no social standing."

"You forget, madam, you are the new Lady Seymour."

"Gammon!"

"But I distinctly remember your saying you meant to use the title."

"With innkeepers and butchers, to insure better rooms and choicer cuts of meat. I never meant to foist myself upon society."

"Nonetheless, you *are* the widow of the eighth Baron Seymour."

"Must I remind you, sir, that the circumstances of my

marriage will not withstand even the most casual scrutiny? And just look at me," she instructed, lifting the sleeve of her dress for his examination, "the widow in green. I should offend all the proprieties."

"A few days ago, you said you cared little for such conventions."

"I know what I said. But at that time, I had only my own destiny to consider. The future of a young girl is quite another matter. I do not wish to have your sister's ostracism from society upon my conscience."

"I do not think that will happen. But in that unlikely event, what if I promised that no blame would be laid at your door?"

"I would say you are talking fustian, because—" She stopped. "Oh, no. I will not debate the issue with you. That is how you outflanked me before, when I did not wish to marry your cousin. First you presented a totally unsuitable plan, then after I said I would not cooperate with you and stated my quite reasonable objections, you backed me into a corner and used my own words against me."

"*I?* Of a certainty, madam, you have your facts confused. Or is it your philosophies? Did you not, fewer than thirty hours ago, inform me that I had nothing whatever to do with your altered circumstances? Correct me if I am wrong, but I believe you credited the whole to heavenly intervention."

"See. That is exactly what I mean. You turn even my own beliefs against me."

"Mea culpa," he said, though the words were spoken so quietly Emaline wondered later if she had merely imagined them.

Neither of them spoke for a time, then very softly he said, "You are right, of course. From almost the first moment I set eyes upon you, I have been entreating you to do things for me and for my family—things that must offend any gently reared female. Things I had no right to ask." He paused. "Will you forgive me?"

A fine blend of contrition and sincerity lent an attractive husky quality to his voice, a huskiness that left Emaline slightly breathless.

In the wake of that breathlessness, her opposition to Liam's plans dissolved like so much morning fog. She sighed, not altogether pleased to have to admit that she was as susceptible as the next hen-witted female to a man's softly spoken apology.

Liam must have taken her sigh for agreement, for immediately he directed the horses to the right, executing a wide circle past the carriage entrance to Westminster Abbey. As the curricle turned and began to retrace its route toward St. James's, Emaline spun around on the seat to snatch a glimpse of the famed Gothic structure as it disappeared in the background. Within seconds, the Abbey's flying buttresses and gabled transepts, with their traceried rose windows, were little more than a blur.

"You have driven past it," she stated accusingly, happy to have something other than Liam's husky voice upon which to concentrate. "So much for your avowed appreciation of ladies who know their own minds. I was well and truly taken in by your fine words, but I might have known your solicitousness regarding my preferences was all a hum."

After encouraging the grays to a trot, Liam turned upon Emaline a smile of such sweetness that she was unable to determine if the steady clop-clop she heard was the sound of the horses' hooves upon the pavement or the loud beating of her own heart as it tried to escape the confines of her chest.

"I will honor my word another day," he promised. "Poet's Corner and the royal monuments will still be there when we return. At this moment, however, I think it wisest that I strike while the iron is hot."

The proverbial iron had cooled off considerably by the time Lord Seymour and his sister entered the drawing room of the Grosvenor Square town house, but Emaline's cheeks were still warm enough to do a creditable job as stand-in.

The entire time he was gone—he had returned to Grillon's Hotel, where he had hired a suite for Miss Cordia and her maid, then brought the young lady back to meet her new relative—Emaline had reproached herself for her earlier foolishness. She had acted like the veryest widgeon, she decided. A peagoose. A ninnyhammer. And all because Liam Whitcomb had smiled at her.

Foolish beyond permission. A woman of seven and twenty should know better! And yet, no man had ever smiled at her in just that way, making her heart feel as though it had turned over in her chest, nor had any man's voice ever made her wonder if she had forgotten how to breathe.

Emaline was still lost in that recollection when Lord Seymour and Miss Cordia Whitcomb were announced.

"Lady Seymour," Liam said, upon entering the drawing room, "may I present my sister? Cordia," he said, turning to the young lady whose hand rested on his arm, "I make you known to Lady Seymour."

On first observing the newcomer, Emaline saw only a pretty girl with thick, dark curls and bright blue eyes, a young lady blessed with a complexion as soft and perfect as a new rose petal and a trim youthful figure. On second glance, however, she discovered that whatever she may have envisioned previously, Miss Cordia was not it.

The young lady who stood before her was a far cry from the shy, quiet child Liam had led her to expect. In fact, she was looking Emaline over from head to toe, a speculative light in her eyes, almost as though she were assessing her for some important position—a position Emaline felt certain had nothing to do with chaperoning. What it did have to do with, she could not even guess. But whatever it was, she obviously passed the test, for the chit had the audacity to wink at her.

"How do you do?" she said, dropping a curtsey. "I am pleased to make your acquaintance, Cousin."

"Call me Emaline," she said, stepping forward to shake the saucy minx's hand. "I insist."

Cordia's smile was the one thing that reminded Emaline of Liam. While she studied brother and sister, who sat side by side upon a small settee, she decided that save for the smile they looked no more alike than two visitors who chanced to meet at the drawing room of a friend. And it was not just the difference in their coloring; it was something more basic. Something in their souls.

Cordia was like a new flower, awaiting with absolute trust that moment when she would unfurl her petals and bask in the warm sunshine her sheltered world would provide. While Liam was like the rolling hills of Wiltshire. Strong. Dependable. Yet all too aware of the destructive ways of man and nature. He understood the vulnerability of all creatures, and as a result, he was protective of the little flower. Of all the little flowers.

How Emaline knew this, she could not say. It was

strange, this feeling of having looked inside another's soul, and yet she was convinced of the truth of her observation. Stranger still was the yearning deep inside her to protect the protector.

"I have a suggestion," Emaline said, once the few minutes of required general conversation had been accomplished. "A plan I believe will accommodate your need for the company of an older person, without undermining your chances for a successful season should the *ton* decide I am not acceptable."

"Not acceptable? But how could that be?" Miss Cordia asked. "You are my cousin's wife. What could be more proper?"

Emaline cast a quick glance at Liam before returning her attention to the young lady. "I have no idea what Lord Seymour may have told you regarding my marriage to your cousin, but—"

"I told her nothing," Liam said.

"Then I shall say only that my marriage was of brief duration and quite unconventional. There may be among the society hostesses some high sticklers who will take exception to both the unseemly haste of my wedding and the fact that I have chosen not to observe a proper period of mourning. If this should happen, and I am known to be your chaperone, the displeasure of those hostesses may be visited upon you. I would not like to think that *on dits* about me had ruined your season."

Miss Cordia's eyes flashed angrily, her pretty face taking on a determined look that was so reminiscent of her brother's, Emaline was hard pressed not to laugh.

"I should jolly well like to see anyone gossip about you!" the young lady declared indignantly.

"Well, I should not," Emaline replied. "And though I

thank you for your championing, that is just what I do not wish to happen. If people talk about me, I do not want you to feel called upon to defend me."

She heard Liam chuckle. "Does that mean that duels are ruled out as well? I am really quite a good shot, if I do say so myself, and I am quite ready to put a hole through anyone you may wish to see ventilated."

"D . . . Duels are most especially ruled out," Emaline answered with as much calm as she could muster. Though she knew he had spoken in jest, the thought that a gentleman might fight a duel in her defense appealed to a latent romantic streak in her, causing a warmth to steal up her neck. Forcing her thoughts back to the subject at hand, she explained to Cordia about her short-lived employment.

"My sole reason for taking a position as paid companion was the opportunity it would afford me to see a bit of the town and enjoy a few of its entertainments. Totally unexceptional diversions, you understand. Plays, museums, that sort of thing."

Miss Cordia tsk-tsked, sympathetic to plans gone awry. "And you have done none of these things?"

Emaline cast an ironic glance at Liam. "I saw a bit of Westminster Abbey."

The object of her sarcasm returned her look with one of studied blandness. "A bit was a sufficient, I assure you." Then, looking around him at the unappealing drawing room, he remarked dryly, "One mausoleum looks much like another."

Hard pressed to keep her lips from betraying her amusement at the remark, Emaline returned the conversation to Miss Cordia. "What I propose, my dear, is that you and the estimable Mrs. Pruett pay me a visit here at Grosvenor Square. For . . . shall we say, four weeks? Mrs. Pruett can remain your titular chaperone, and while she rests her broken limb, you and I will visit the shops and perhaps some of the sights."

She looked at the girl's beaming face. "What say you to that plan?"

"Oh, ma'am," she replied eagerly. "It is the very thing!"

Several minutes later Emaline and Liam stood in the vestibule, waiting for Cordia, who had gone abovestairs with Hannah to see which of the guest bedrooms would serve for the recuperating Mrs. Pruett. While they waited, Liam asked once again if Emaline did not wish to reconsider his offer to remove to Cavendish Square. "For I am persuaded the house I rented there for the little season will provide a degree of comfort not to be found here at Seymour House."

Emaline shook her head. "If I am to act as hostess to my cousin, I cannot do so in her home. And as you reminded me yesterday, this house—at least for the moment—is mine."

"Very well," he replied. "I will, of course, see to the expenses." When he noted the blush that stained her cheeks, he added, "It will matter little to me at which establishment my sister resides, for she will cost me no more at Grosvenor Square than at Cavendish."

"You are very tactful," Emaline said softly, "to present it to me in such a sensible light. I wish I could refuse your offer, but you and I both know that I cannot."

"Then do not do so," he said, admiring the soft curve, yet stubborn lift, of her chin as her pride fought with her more practical side. "And while we are on the subject, I should also inform you that I have opened accounts at most of the better shops. You and Cordia should have no trouble purchasing what you need."

Her chin came up a little more. "But I require nothing."

"Believe me, you will once you start bear-leading my sister. Cordia desires to see and do it all, and if I know anything of the matter, she will also wish to change her costume before each new activity."

"That may be so, but I—"

"You, madam, have been so obliging as to promise to keep up with her. And though you may not believe me now, I predict that you will soon tire of wearing the same dress day after day and wish to have a few alternatives in your clothespress. Even though," he added quietly, "the frock you are wearing is vastly becoming. Did I mention what that particular shade of green does to your eyes?"

She shook her head.

"It brings out their hidden depths. Their mystery."

At his words, she lowered her gold-tipped lashes, then moments later she raised them . . . slowly, almost provocatively. When she finally granted him a full view of the sable-brown orbs, they had become suddenly playful. "Are you offering me a *carte blanche,* sir?"

"Minx," he accused, unable to shift his gaze from those teasing eyes. "You know me better than that."

"Perhaps. But you do not know me. How can you be certain that I will not seize the main chance and order dozens of new costumes." Her look was bold, challenging. "I might bankrupt you."

His laughter echoed in the small vestibule. "Madam, you have my permission to try."

Chapter 8

It was on the third day of a veritable orgy of shopping that Emaline saw Geoffrey Beauchamp. She very nearly did not recognize him, however, for he was dressed not in his pretty Hussar's uniform but in a handsomely cut morning coat of Spanish blue—a shade that complemented to perfection his crisp dark hair and his sun-bronzed face.

She and Cordia had only just come from a fitting at Madame Julienne's, on Oxford Street, and were preparing to step into a hackney carriage when she heard someone speak her name.

"Lady Seymour," he said, removing his beaver and executing a graceful bow. "Well met, ma'am."

"Captain Beauchamp. How do you do?"

"Obviously, not very well," he said, placing his gloved hand over his heart as though that organ had sustained a telling blow. "For when last we met, you called me Champ. Do not, I pray you, be so cruel as to return to odious formality."

Emaline chuckled. "I would not think of it, sir. From this moment on we shall conduct ourselves as two old friends, but do permit me to stretch formality just long enough to present you to my guest. Cordia," she said, gaining the young lady's attention, "there is someone here I wish you to meet."

"Did you say *Cordia?* Liam's sister? I—"

As Miss Whitcomb turned from the coach, her pretty face no longer hidden by the wide poke of her pale pink bonnet, the gentleman's mouth dropped open, while at the same time he seemed to lose the power of speech.

Fortunately, the object of his awe was made of sterner stuff, and she hesitated but a fraction of a second before finding her voice. "You can be none other than Champ." Smiling charmingly, she extended her hand. "How pleased I am to meet you at last, for I have heard tales past counting of the escapades got up to by you and my brother."

Recovering his composure, the gentleman took the hand she offered, holding it as though it were fashioned of delicate porcelain. "Your servant, Miss Whitcomb."

In the midst of this exchange, the gentleman's name was spoken by a soft-voiced young lady who waited over near the entrance to Madame Julienne's, her eyes cast downward, her youthful cheeks pink with embarrassment.

"Yes?" he answered distractedly. Then, looking behind him as if only just recalling that they stood on a public street, he beckoned to the speaker. "Forgive me, my dear, I forgot you were there."

Emaline had no difficulty in guessing the identity of the modestly, though expensively dressed, young lady. Such lack of gallantry from a man of Captain Beauchamp's stamp must always denote the presence of a sister. And the dark hair, the gray eyes, the slightly pointed chin—softer, more feminine versions of Champ's own features—convinced Emaline that this was indeed Miss Mary Beauchamp.

When introductions were completed all around, nothing

would suit the gentleman but that they should allow him to treat them all to ices at Gunther's. "My mother is laid upon her bed, a victim of the migraine," he informed them, "so I have been squiring my sister from shop to shop for the better part of the morning. As a result, I find myself very much in need of refreshment."

The sweet, cooked-sugar smell of the famous confectioner's shop permeated the air as they took their seats around the small round table, and since laughter and joviality were the order of the day, the foursome were soon on a first-name basis. It was not to be wondered at that a party including two such gregarious creatures as Captain Beauchamp and Miss Whitcomb was a great success.

While they awaited the arrival of their ices, Champ and Cordia regaled them with stories of some of Liam's most celebrated boyhood pranks. And though Emaline could add little to the discourse, she found the subject matter of more than passing interest. After a time, however, she thought it only polite to include Miss Mary Beauchamp in the conversation.

"And what of you, Mary? Have you no scandalous reminiscences of your brother with which to entertain us?"

Miss Mary, a timid young lady of barely seventeen summers, blushed to the very roots of her hair. "No, ma'am."

"I vow," Cordia protested jovially, "'tis not fair. You must confide in us, Mary. And do not, I pray you, try to fob us off with some faradiddle about Champ being an exemplary young man, for neither Emaline nor I will believe it."

While Champ gave his rapt attention to a dusky curl that had fallen across Cordia's forehead, Miss Beauchamp gave her attention to her clasped hands, where they lay in her lap. "He was used to bring me sweets in a paper twist," she said quietly, "when he came home on holiday. And the summer I had the chicken pox, he came up to the nursery each afternoon and played skittles with me."

The gentleman, having only just realized what his sister was relating, spun around to stare at her, horror writ plainly upon his handsome face. "By Jove, Mary."

"And that time I sprained my wrist, he—"

"Have done, there's a good girl," begged her brother, his voice gruff with embarrassment. "Boring stuff, my dear, I assure you." Then turning to Cordia, he said, "I was twelve when she was born." As though the age difference both explained and excused everything.

For Emaline's part, she found the young lady's revelations charming. "I was an only child," she told her, "so I envy you having an older brother. As for you, Champ," she reproved gently, "I envy you for being blessed with such a loyal little sister."

Neither Emaline nor Cordia suspected just how fortuitous was their meeting with Captain and Miss Beauchamp. Not, that is, until the next day, when a letter addressed to Lady Seymour was hand delivered by a footman wearing bordeaux and silver livery.

"Who is it from?" Cordia asked, looking up from her perusal of *The Ladies' Monthly Museum*.

It being the Sabbath, the two ladies had spent the hours since returning from church lounging about in the ground-floor drawing room, recouping their strength from the last few days of nonstop shopping. Emaline occupied a comfortably stuffed, velvet wing chair, while Cordia reclined upon a beige brocade settee, her stockinged feet propped upon a tapestried footstool, her kid slippers kicked off and lost somewhere beneath a pile of fashion periodicals strewn about the carpet.

That the drawing room was hardly recognizable as the same chamber Liam had referred to as a mausoleum was due to several sessions of hard labor on Emaline's part. With Turner's and Hannah's help, she had weeded out most of the heavy, masculine pieces of furniture, replacing them with a pair of elegant gold chairs, in the rococo French taste of the previous century, and an exquisite George I writing bureau, all of which had been found in the attic, hidden beneath Holland covers.

Once the remaining furniture had been rearranged, and the heavy red damask drapes had been removed from the double set of French windows, the room had displayed an unexpected charm. It had wanted only the unsealing of the windows to let in a breath of fresh air, then all similarity to a mausoleum was banished. In fact, the drawing room had become a favorite gathering place, and even the fastidious Mrs. Pruett, during one of her infrequent sojourns belowstairs, had declared it a quite tolerable chamber.

Turning slightly in her chair, so that more light fell upon the letter, Emaline broke the seal and opened the single sheet of paper. Going immediately to the signature at the bottom of the page, she said, "It is signed, Phoebe Beauchamp."

"Lady Phoebe?"

Cordia tossed her periodical aside and came to sit on the floor at Emaline's feet, urging her friend to read the missive quickly. "For I am positively agog to know what she can have written."

Equally curious, Emaline read the neatly written lines. "We are invited to tea," she said. "The Beauchamp landau will call for us at four of the clock."

* * *

Emaline stood at the dining room window, observing the different carriages that traversed Brook Street en route to and from the park. Though the ormolu clock on the mantel had only just struck the half-hour, she had been dressed and waiting for several minutes, having come down early especially to watch for the arrival of Lady Phoebe's carriage.

As it transpired, the first vehicle to pull up at the curb before number seventeen was not the landau but Liam's curricle, with the owner seated upon the box, the ribbons laced comfortably between his fingers. Emaline found herself staring at him, noting his posture—military yet never stiff—and admiring the way he controlled the horses—firmly, yet with a respect for their nobility and spirit.

Watching him toss the ribbons to the groom, then leap from the curricle as effortlessly as though the sporting carriage stood mere inches above the ground, she spared a moment to appreciate his agility and manly grace. And if that appreciation took the form of a flutter inside her chest that put from her mind all thoughts of elegant landaus and invitations to tea, she cared not one whit, for she realized now what had made the last few days seem so tame.

She had not seen Liam since Wednesday, and though her time had been filled to capacity with the myriad tasks necessary for the outfitting of a young lady about to make her come-out, the busy days had been like a stew served without the proper condiments—filling but flavorless. She wondered why she had not realized it before.

Almost as if he felt her watching him, Liam glanced up toward the window. Embarrassed lest he discover her gawking at him, Emaline stepped back out of view. As she moved, she gave the skirt of her new manilla carriage dress a twitch, just in case the russet-corded flounce had gotten caught on the top of her jean half-boots, and as she did so, she suddenly realized that Liam would be the first to view her in her new finery. For some reason, she found that fact inordinately pleasing.

After placing upon her head a small straw bonnet trimmed with russet quilling and short feathers, she took a moment to tie the wide satin ribbons not beneath her chin, but at a jaunty angle near her ear as the milliner had shown her. Then, confident that she looked her best, she opened the dining room door and waited just inside the threshold while Turner admitted the visitor.

"Good afternoon, my lord," the butler said.

"Good day, Turner." Handing over his hat and driving gloves, Liam asked if the ladies were at home.

"They are, sir."

"I am in luck, then, for I have come unannounced and without invitation. Will you please ask Lady Seymour if she can spare me a few moments of her time? I have something in particular I wish to discuss with—"

Turning so that he spied her poised there in the doorway, Liam fell silent. Even after he took several steps toward her, he offered her no word of greeting. He merely stared at her, pinning her with those dark blue eyes and compelling her to let him look his fill. His entire focus was on her, and as Emaline stood quietly, lost in the moment, a lightness assailed her limbs, making her wonder if her knees might give way beneath her. Liam stepped closer, still saying nothing, letting the force of his gaze speak for him.

He stood so near she could feel his warm breath stir one of the bonnet's feathers at her temple. Then, as though it were the most natural thing in the world, he reached out with both hands and gave the saucily tied bow a gentle adjustment. "There," he said. "Now you are perfect."

When he released the bow, the knuckles of his right hand brushed against her cheek. Softly. Gently. And though his fingers lingered scarcely more than an instant, his touch sent little sparks to ignite the nerves of her flesh, bringing her skin to life. Emaline could not breathe. She could not take her eyes from his. And if her very life had depended upon it, she could not have moved away from him.

She had wanted sparks. All her adult life she had yearned for them, and now that they were hers for the taking, she stood like a mesmerized rabbit, unable to move. Unable to speak. She wanted desperately to respond, to encourage him to touch her again, but she was uncertain what to do.

From somewhere in the recesses of her brain, she recalled the second lesson from the little book taken from the vitrine. *Make him aware of your mouth,* the author had instructed. Unfortunately, the balance of the instruction remained lost inside Emaline's head, and she could not remember how that feat was to be accomplished.

Improvising, she moistened her lips with the tip of her tongue, hoping the light might reflect upon the moisture and give her mouth an appealing iridescence. The maneuver worked better than she could have hoped.

Liam caught his breath, and as he stared at her lips, his eyes darkened with an emotion Emaline had never seen before. Something within her responded to that emotion, however, and as if driven to do so, she lifted her face, offering it to him to do with as he wished.

"Emaline!" Cordia called from the top of the stair. "The landau is here. I saw it from my window. Emaline? Where are you?"

Startled, Emaline stepped away from Liam. Somehow

she managed to answer, "I am here," when in all honesty, she wished to yell, "Go away, I wish you were *not* here."

"There you are," Cordia said, fairly floating down the steps, the pale primrose of her tea gown repeated in a simple bandeau that was threaded charmingly through her curls. "And you here, too, Liam. Wonderful. Has Emaline told you where we are bound? I hope not, for I do so want to see the surprise in your face."

"Emaline has not uttered a single word," he said.

From the evenness of his voice, one might be forgiven for suspecting that he had not been as moved as Emaline by what had almost happened between them.

Or had it almost happened?

Some primal awareness deep inside Emaline had told her that Liam meant to kiss her. But what if she had been mistaken? What if only *she* had wanted it? Had she made a fool of herself? No longer confident in her assessment of the situation, embarrassment burned her cheeks.

While Emaline fought a wish to run from the room, the irrepressible Miss Cordia came forward, a pert grin upon her face. "You will never guess our destination, Liam."

"Since you have declared me defeated even before I try my luck, I shall refrain from suggesting the Taj Mahal or the catacombs of Rome."

"Pooh," said the young lady, "as though anyone would wish to go to such dreary places."

"I stand corrected. It is as you say; I have not a guess."

"We are bound for Pall Mall," she declared triumphantly. "We are to take tea with Lady Phoebe Beauchamp."

"Beauchamp!" Liam looked at Emaline, the warmth that had been in his eyes only moments ago now turned to chips of blue ice. "So, my lady. Champ has made good his promise to seek you out."

Still riddled with doubt regarding their earlier encounter, Emaline spoke more sharply than she intended. "You introduced him to me, sir. Surely you can have no objection to the acquaintance."

"Of course he has not," the gentleman's sister answered for him. "Liam and Champ have been friends for years out of mind. Why should he cavil at our enjoying Champ's company?"

"Why indeed?" her brother muttered.

Lady Phoebe was every inch the earl's daughter. A tall, slender woman of about fifty, her silver-streaked dark hair and her gray eyes were so like those of her son and daughter that Emaline felt she would have known her for their mother if she had chanced upon her on a crowded street. Not that there was the least possibility of ever encountering Lady Phoebe in such a place! One look at her unyielding posture and her fixed smile, and one knew immediately that the daughter of the Earl of Chartier did not mingle with the masses.

Having been reared on the principle of noblesse oblige, Lady Phoebe knew her worth and expected all those from the lesser orders to appreciate it without need of instruction. Still, having invited the two ladies into her home for tea, their hostess was unfailingly polite. Oddly enough, this latter trait annoyed Emaline more than outright snobbery would have done.

"So," Lady Phoebe began after Champ and the two very young ladies had quit the opulent drawing room in favor of a walk in the back garden, "I collect that I am to wish you happy and extend my condolences at one and the same time."

Unable to think of any constructive reply to such a comment, Emaline chose to ignore it, resorting instead to sipping from the delicate bone china teacup she held in her hands. What her ladyship thought of such a breach of etiquette, her guest neither knew nor cared.

"Please," her hostess urged when the maid passed the plate of sugared sponge cakes a second time, "have another. Cook makes them especially for my son, who has been a favorite with all the servants since his schoolboy days. Any time she knows he is expected for tea, we are all obliged to partake of the sweet whether we wish it or not."

Emaline smiled politely but declined the treat, wishing for only one thing—that the favorite of the servants would not be overlong in his stroll in the garden. City gardens were of necessity small; surely it would not take long to traverse the whole.

With no desire for a protracted *tête-à-tête* with Champ's mother, Emaline glanced toward the door of the elegantly appointed first-floor drawing room, trying what she could to *will* the return of the threesome. To her disappointment, the only time the door opened was to allow the maid to exit the room.

"Now," Lady Phoebe said, setting her cup on the handsome rosewood teapoy just to the left of her chair, "we may speak more freely."

"Freely?" Taking her cue from her hostess, Emaline set her teacup aside as well, the contents no more than tasted. "I am sure I do not know what you mean, ma'am."

"I refer to this marriage of yours," she replied. "As far as I can discover, no one in town knew of Lord Seymour's plans to remarry. Not that I had more than a nodding acquaintance with the man, you understand, but still, this failure to announce the wedding in the papers gives it a decidedly havy-cavy appearance."

"Do you think so, ma'am? I own I had not given the matter much thought."

In truth, Emaline had given it a great deal of thought, and though she had a story ready to hand, she felt disinclined to relate it to this stranger who seemed to believe it within her rights to demand answers.

"Come, come," Lady Phoebe prompted. "Do not dissemble. I must and will get to the bottom of this, for it is of some importance to me."

Importance? Emaline did not see how this could be so, but short of being pointedly rude to the older woman, she could not refuse to offer some sort of answer.

"Ambrose asked me to marry him, and at the urging of his heir, I accepted his hand. It was as simple as that. Nothing particularly noteworthy. I had just lost my parent, and the first Lady Seymour was an old friend of my mother's; for this reason, all the parties concerned thought the marriage a good idea. After a time I acquiesced to their pleading."

Continuing with the blend of truth and fiction that was becoming more distasteful to her as the story progressed, Emaline said, "Ours was not a love match, but rather a *marriage de convenance*. Very shortly after the wedding, my husband died. Perhaps no one thought it necessary to inform the world of either circumstance. I neither knew nor cared. Nor, if you will excuse what must appear bad manners on my part, do I wish to discuss the matter further." She tried for a convincing sniff, hoping it would end the catechism. "I should not wish to embarrass myself by becoming lachrymose."

"Your reticence does you credit," her inquisitor said. "Allow me to prolong your distress only long enough to express my hope that your husband left you adequately provided for. A gel of your spirit will not wish to hang upon the new Lord Seymour's sleeve."

Emaline gasped. Even from an earl's daughter, this questioning had crossed the line. "I assure you," she answered stiffly, "you need have no concern on my behalf. I am amply provided for by my grandfather, Sir Gerald Conklin."

Her ladyship appeared inordinately pleased at this piece of information. "How fortuitous, my dear. I congratulate you upon the foresight of your grandparent."

Though Emaline pressed her lips together, only just containing her anger at such an invasion of her privacy, Lady Phoebe smiled, either unaware of or uninterested in Emaline's sensibilities. "While the young people are still in the garden," she continued, neatly relegating Emaline to her own middle-aged status, "there is a matter I wish to discuss with you."

"I had supposed there might be, ma'am." Although she had not a clue as to what her hostess wished to say, it had not taken Emaline much above a half-dozen minutes after entering the salon to detemine that their invitation to tea had not been extended solely for the pleasure of their company.

"I wish to speak with you of Miss Mary Beauchamp."

Rightly discerning that the earl's daughter did not mean this to be a two-sided conversation, Emaline refrained from needless comment, merely hoping that their coze would soon be interrupted.

"You cannot have helped but noticed, Lady Seymour, that my daughter is a rather shy miss. I had hoped that she might grow out of it, that she would one day show some sign of the liveliness that is so much a part of my son, Geoffrey's, makeup, but so far that has not happened."

Emaline resisted an almost overwhelming urge to inform her hostess that Miss Mary Beauchamp showed much greater liveliness when not in the shadow of her overbearing mother.

"Still," said the young lady's parent, "she is my only daughter, and though she is blessed with neither wit nor any great degree of beauty, I wish to see her well established. That is, of course, the reason I invited you here today."

For one horrible moment, Emaline thought she was about to be pressed into service once again as a chaperone. She was disabused of that fanciful notion almost immediately.

"You can imagine my delight, Lady Seymour, when I heard that Mary and Geoffrey had made Miss Cordia Whitcomb's acquaintance. And yours, too, of course."

"Of course," Emaline replied dryly.

Lady Phoebe inclined her head ever so slightly, as though indicating her willingness to entertain occasional responses.

"As you may know," she continued, "my son and Liam Whitcomb have been friends since their days at Eton, and though Liam was from an unexceptional family—though, as his father's heir, not without interesting prospects—I never considered him as a possible applicant for my daughter's hand. Naturally, now that he has succeeded to his cousin's dignities, the circumstances are quite different."

Emaline was certain her mouth fell open. "Your pardon, Lady Phoebe, if I appear a bit of a lackwit myself, but has Li—that is to say, Lord Seymour—asked for Miss Beauchamp's hand?"

"Not yet. How could he? They have not, so far, been introduced. With your assistance, however, I mean to remedy that circumstance. They will, naturally, require a reasonable amount of time in which to become better acquainted, but I see no reason why Mary's father and I could not announce our daughter's betrothal by the end of the little season. And since I have never been an advocate of long engagements, I believe a Christmas wedding should serve. In that way," concluded the devoted mother, "I may wash my hands of the entire matter and get on with my own life."

So surprised was Emaline by this dispassionate statement that she had trouble containing her resentment of the shy young lady's mother. The woman spoke as though she were offering cattle for auction at the local fair.

"You seem to have it all worked out, Lady Phoebe, and try as I may, I cannot comprehend how I would be of the least assistance to you in your plans. Nor, for that matter, why I should wish to be."

"Because," she answered, as though explaining a basic principle of mathematics to one incapable of grasping the most fundamental of precepts, "I am prepared to introduce both you and Lord Seymour's sister to society. In exchange for my patronage—a not insignificant offering, as you must know—all I ask of you is that you take Mary up with you as often as possible, so that she may come in Liam's way. After they have become acquainted, you may then leave all to me. When I feel the time is right, I will broach the subject of marriage with his lordship."

Staring at the woman, and unable to credit the sheer audacity of her proposal, Emaline wondered what Liam would say if he knew his future had been so neatly planned and tied up by his self-appointed mother-in-law-to-be?

Lady Phoebe obviously considered both the conversation and the visit at an end, for she rang the bell for the maid, instructed the girl to tell John Coachman to bring the landau around, then she gave Emaline two limp fingers to shake.

"My daughter and Lord Seymour will make a perfect match," she said by way of farewell. "I am certain you can see that."

Emaline wanted to deny it. She wanted to tell the arrogant woman to her face that Liam deserved better—that he was kind and generous and brave, and that he had earned the right to a life of love and happiness. As she descended the wide marble staircase to the ground floor, she longed to punctuate her denial by pulling every last antique vase from its niche in the wall and smashing each one to the floor. But she did not. How could she do so when reason told her that Lady Phoebe—cold fish or not—was correct? From the viewpoint of their world, Liam and Mary were a perfect match. Liam had enormous wealth, and Mary had an impeccable lineage.

"The stuff of true romance!" Emaline said. Then, to the surprise of the footman who waited beside the entrance door, she followed this cynical observation by muttering a word no well-born lady should even know existed.

Chapter 9

The servants at Seymour House took their half-days on Sunday, so Emaline and Cordia made do that evening with the lemonade and sandwiches left for them in the drawing room. It was not to be wondered at that while they enjoyed this light repast, Cordia beguiled the time with repeated references to the Beauchamp town house, the Beauchamp furniture, the Beauchamp garden, and even the Beauchamp servants' livery, declaring them all absolute perfection.

"Do you not agree, Emaline?"

"Of a certainty," her auditor answered promptly, if with somewhat less enthusiasm.

That the young lady assiduously avoided any mention of the Beauchamp heir, and blushed furiously each time Emaline spoke his name, was more telling of her interest in that direction than all her rhapsodizing over the *things* she had admired.

"And Lady Phoebe," she added. "Was her ladyship not kindness itself to invite us back tomorrow to meet Lady Sefton?"

Apparently not noticing that her companion failed to answer this last question, Cordia continued with unabated enthusiasm. "Almack's! Only think of it. If Lady Sefton approves of us, we will receive vouchers to the Assembly Rooms." She sighed contentedly. "Is not everything coming about beautifully? And all, I might add, without the least need of assistance from Mrs. Pruett. I declare, I find this entire business much easier than she led me to believe. Without lifting a finger we have had tea with an earl's daughter, and now we are to meet one of the patronesses of Almack's."

Emaline let her continue in her misreading of the situation. What good would it do her to know that this marked attention from Lady Phoebe came at a high price? Or that the woman's introducing them to the kindest and most mature of the seven patronesses was not an act of friendship but of barter?

Not that Emaline had agreed to Lady Phoebe's plan to introduce Mary to Liam's notice. Actually, she had resolved neither to help nor to hinder the scheme. As in all things, she would act as she had been taught by her dear father, and leave the outcome to heaven. Mary Beauchamp was a gentle, unprepossessing young lady, and if Cordia wished to include her in their outings, Emaline would not say her nay. On the other hand, she meant never to suggest the inclusion of anyone.

If, by chance, Mary and Liam should meet at Seymour House, Emaline would treat them with the courtesy and respect due any guest in her home. As for entering into Lady Beauchamp's conspiracy, however, Emaline would not be a party to it.

"What think you of the pink with the white volens? Will it do for tomorrow?"

Calling herself to attention, Emaline gave it as her opinion that anything Cordia chose to wear would look charming. Since this was no more than the truth, it mattered little that she had no idea to which of her new dresses the young lady referred.

A moment later Cordia recalled a pair of kidskin gloves she had purchased at Grafton House on Friday, and thinking they might do very nicely with the dress, she excused herself and ran up to her bedchamber to make certain the pinks were of similar hue. She had no more than left the room when the knocker sounded on the front door. Because the servants were from home, Emaline was obliged to answer the summons herself, though she could not imagine who would be calling at seven of the clock on a Sabbath evening.

The caller was Liam.

The moment she saw him, her heart's pace quickened noticeably, a circumstance, she told herself, that owed everything to his having called at an unusual hour and nothing whatever to the fact that he stood before her resplendent in beautifully cut evening clothes that fit his slender form to perfection.

Emaline was forced to swallow before she could speak. "Is ought amiss?"

"Nothing is wrong," he replied, removing his silk hat and stepping inside the vestibule. "Nothing, that is, if you disallow the fact that I called this afternoon for an express purpose, but left without having accomplished my errand."

Having said this, he set his hat on the ebony console just to the left of the door, then reached inside his mulberry coat and removed the black leather jeweler's box. "According to the terms of my cousin's will, I believe this property is yours."

Bowing slightly, he presented the box to Emaline in much the same manner as she had presented it to him on the morning of his Cousin Ambrose's funeral. Her reaction to it was much the same as his had been.

"I do not understand, sir. Why have you brought the ruby necklace back to me?"

"As to that," he said, a look on his face that was part amusement, part chagrin, "I have and I have not."

"Again, sir, I do not understand. Could you, perhaps, be a little less cryptic?"

"Forgive me. What I should have said is that I have brought back the necklace, but I have *not* brought back rubies. The reason being, this necklace is paste."

"Paste! Are you sure?"

"The experts at Rundell and Bridges are quite certain. I took a ride over to Ludgate Hill yesterday morning for verification."

Liam opened the box so that the dark red gems were visible, and though Emaline trusted him regarding their genuineness—or lack thereof—it was difficult to credit the fact when they sparkled so beautifully in the light from the chandelier.

"Paste, you say."

He nodded. "The real ruby necklace, of which this is a first-rate copy, is in the safe at Whitcomb Hall, where it has lain since my mother wore it last. That was at least a dozen years ago."

"Now I truly do not understand. Did you know when I gave you this necklace that it was a copy?"

"I certainly hoped it was. Especially since I had not seen the original for years and had no knowledge that a copy had ever been made."

"Your father never told you?"

Liam shook his head. "My father never knew. He had the original made as a gift for my mother to commemorate the birth of my sister. The paste copy was never commissioned by him."

"Then who would do so? And why? According to Lady Seymour's note to my mother, she found the necklace in *her own* safe at Seymour Park. She thought it a gift intended for her, something her husband meant as a surprise."

"But a surprise for whom?" Liam asked quietly.

He closed the jeweler's box with a snap, then set it on the console. "I can offer you proof of nothing—neither the *who* nor the *why*—only conjecture based on something that happened a number of years ago."

Because they still stood in the vestibule where anyone might overhear, he spoke quietly. "Seventeen years ago, a pair of thieves broke into my father's bookroom at Whitcomb Hall. At gunpoint, they forced him to open the safe, then demanded that he hand over the ruby necklace, an item worth in excess of thirty thousand pounds. Father never understood why they wanted only that one piece when other valuable jewelry was there for the taking."

As Emaline pondered the riddle, an uncomfortable suspicion began to take shape in her mind—a surmise that made her wish the necklace still lay undiscovered in her mother's workbox.

"Please assure me," she said, her tone of voice implying her expectation of impending contradiction, "that it was not some scheme of Ambrose's to defraud his own cousin."

"I wish I could do so. Unfortunately, I believe it to be the truth."

"Alas," she said, sighing dramatically, "my deceased husband grows more delightful with each new fact I learn of him. Such an interesting mixture of greed and family disloyalty, do you not agree?"

"I never dispute a lady," he said, smiling at her sarcasm.

"I cannot tell you, sir, how pleased I am to be his widow."

Liam chuckled. "A fortuitous circumstance, to be sure. Especially since it lends such finality to the relationship."

"Oh, but I must disagree. I do not despair of discovering at any moment that Ambrose is wanted for highway robbery, multiple murders, and crimes against the crown. And I shall not marvel at it if, as his widow, I find myself hauled off to prison as his accomplice."

"I sincerely hope it will not come to that," Liam said pleasantly. "But if it should, I want you to know that I will do everything in my power to see that your cell is supplied with fresh straw each and every week."

Laughter rose in Emaline's throat, but she mastered it, saying quite seriously, "Once again, sir, I am overwhelmed by your solicitousness."

He made her a bow. "The least I can do, ma'am. I beg you, think nothing of it."

"Believe me, I shall not. Nor, if I can help it, do I mean to think of your odious cousin."

Returning to the subject of the attempted robbery, Emaline asked, "Do you suppose Ambrose meant to switch the paste for the real necklace; then, after claiming that he had managed to recover it from the thieves, return it to your father, hoping to pass it off as legitimate?"

"Somehow I doubt it. My father was a very knowing man, quite difficult to deceive. A more likely scenario would be that Ambrose planned to dupe the men who physically committed the crime. If he could switch the copy for the original before the thieves tried to sell it, he would not be obliged to split the proceeds with them."

"Charming. Am I supposed to feel better knowing he meant only to cheat his fellow malefactors?"

"Remember, it is mere conjecture on my part. All I know for certain is that when the criminals ran from the bookroom, my father removed a pistol from his desk and fired upon the man holding the necklace. The felon fell to the floor, blood gushing from his leg; unfortunately, his partner in crime fled and was never captured. The real rubies never left the room."

"What happened to the man who was shot?"

"When his wound healed, he was tried and sentenced to twenty years hard labor. Without, I might add, ever naming his co-conspirators."

The mention of hard labor put Emaline in mind of Samuel Turner, the butler's brother, and the story she had meant to tell Liam about the servants being blackmailed by Vernon Brofton, the late Lord Seymour's valet. "That reminds me of something I wished to relate to you. Something I think you should—"

"Liam," Cordia called from the top of the stairs. "How glad I am that you are here. Mrs. Pruett wishes to come downstairs, and I think she would much prefer your arm to mine."

Giving Emaline an apologetic look, he took the steps two at a time, offered his arm to the invalid, and escorted her down the stairs and into the drawing room. When the chaperone was comfortably settled in Emaline's favorite wing chair, with a small tapestried stool beneath her encased leg, Liam excused himself to the ladies, explaining that he was promised to meet friends for supper and a hand of whist.

"I really must go," he told Emaline when she walked him to the front door, "or I shall be late. That thing you wanted to tell me, can it wait until tomorrow?"

"Yes, of course. It has waited this long, it can—Tomorrow? What is tomorrow?"

Liam retrieved his hat from the console, leaving the jeweler's box where he had set it earlier. "Tomorrow," he said, "is our return trip to Westminster Abbey. What say you to eleven?"

Trying to ignore the thrill of excitement that shot through her at the thought of spending the morning with Liam, Emaline said, "My wits must surely have gone begging, sir, for I do not remember your asking me if I would accompany you tomorrow."

"I did not," he agreed affably. "I asked only if eleven was a good time. If, as you believe, you are in imminent danger of being hauled off to prison for my cousin's crimes, there is no time to waste upon such trifles as invitations and acceptances. It is imperative that we go at once."

"Imperative?" she asked, her tone skeptical. "And why is that, pray?"

"Purest logic," he answered innocently. "It will give you something to think about while in your cell."

Emaline made a noise that was part gasp, part chuckle. "Abominable man!"

"Just so," he agreed. "Perhaps you ought not to have married him."

"I meant you!"

"But I protest! My cousin was *much* more abominable than I."

This time she laughed freely. "Let us not split hairs, sir. Obviously the trait runs in the family."

"In all save the females."

"Undoubtedly," she said. "For Cordia is a credit to her lineage."

"Hear, hear. There can be no two opinions on my sister's worth. And now, while we are agreed upon at least one subject, I think it politic of me to take my leave."

When Liam reached out and caught her left wrist, holding it in his firm grasp, Emaline thought he meant to slide his hand beneath her palm and lift her fingers to his lips. To her surprise, he made no move to do so, and while he maintained his hold upon her, his thumb began to trace a pattern of warm delight across her skin. For several moments they stood thus.

Neither of them spoke. He did not; she could not.

When he finally abandoned the sweet stroking torture that made her pulse race with the speed of a thoroughbred horse, he turned her wrist over; then he bent down and placed a soft, lingering kiss upon the pale, sensitive flesh.

"Eleven?" he whispered.

Emaline made some sort of reply. What it was, she had no way of knowing, for her brain had been seared beyond all sane thought by the flame that had burned its way up her arm, then spread like molten fire throughout her body.

"Until then," Liam said.

Still mesmerized by the feel of his lips upon her skin, Emaline stood in the doorway and watched him bound down the steps, then climb up to the box seat of his curricle. The clatter of the carriage wheels upon the pavement had faded into the night before she came to her senses enough to close the door. It was only when she entered the drawing room and heard Cordia regaling Mrs. Pruett with an account of the thrills in store for them the next morning that she remembered their engagement at Pall Mall to meet Lady Sefton.

Emaline passed a most unrestful night. After having excused herself to Cordia and the chaperone on the pretext of a headache, she had gone to her room, seeking a private place in which to sort through her disordered emotions.

As she lay upon her bed, watching the light from a single candle casting soft shadows upon the ceiling, she realized that one thing had already been decided in her head, it needed only to be admitted aloud: She would not go to Pall Mall on the morrow. To do so was to fall in with Lady Phoebe's machinations. Even if she never spoke a word, Emaline's presence in her ladyship's house would be tantamount to giving her consent to aid in Liam's entrapment.

As for Cordia, Emaline need have no concern for that young lady's welfare; Lady Phoebe would hardly cut her if she meant Mary to become her sister-in-law. And even if that had not been the case, Lady Sefton was not likely to refuse a voucher to a pretty-behaved young lady with a lively way about her, especially not one who was also a considerable heiress.

In regard to her own circumstance, Emaline had never any wish to be thrown among society. Of what value was a voucher for Almack's to her? In four weeks, when she received her quarter-day money, she would return to Wiltshire. Until that time, her goal was the same as it had always been, to enjoy her sojourn in the city.

Her heart beat a little faster at the recollection that her enjoyment was to be enhanced by Liam's driving her to Westminster Abbey. That decision had already been made as well. From the moment he mentioned the outing, she had never any intention of saying him nay.

As she thought of Liam, the inside of her wrist grew warm once again, almost as if his lips were still pressed against her flesh. Hoping she might recapture the wonderful sensations he had sent through her body, Emaline lifted her arm and pressed the wrist to her mouth, as though she might transfer his kiss to her lips.

While Liam had bent over her hand, she had wished for

the kiss to go on forever. As well, she had longed to reach out her other hand to his head, to let her fingertips explore the golden radiance the candlelight cast upon his thick, straight hair. It had seemed like magic, the way the light from the chandelier had shimmered upon the dark blond strands. Like moonlight reflected on the white sand of a tropical shore.

Strange how such a simple thing could cause a yearning deep within her. She sighed. The kiss, his touch, they had ignited a passion inside her, an almost overwhelming longing to know more.

As she recalled how handsome he had appeared in his evening clothes, the longing became an ache. He had looked so strong, so full of life, and she had burned with a desire to know how it would feel to be wrapped in his arms, to experience the joy of being encompassed by his energy. She wanted to know that and more. She wanted to feel Liam's lips explore her mouth.

Lost in her imagination, she almost failed to hear the soft knock at her bedroom door. When Cordia spoke, Emaline jumped guiltily.

"Are you asleep?"

"No. Not yet."

Stepping inside the room, the young lady said, "I came to see if you wished a tisane for your headache."

Ashamed of herself for having resorted to such a blatant falsehood, Emaline muttered something about sleep being the best medicine.

"An undisputable truth," Cordia answered. Then, without being invited to do so, she walked over to the stand-up looking glass, absently rearranging a curl that fell back among its fellows the moment she released it. While she busied her hands with straightening Emaline's silver comb and brush set, she asked rather nonchalantly why Liam thought it necessary to call twice in one day. "Was there something particular he needed to say to you?"

Emaline did not wish to discuss Liam with his sister, for Cordia was as sharp as she could stare, and she might discover something that Emaline did not wish anyone to know. Having only just acknowledged her own feelings, and not at all certain that Liam shared any of those sentiments, she did not wish to be exposed to anyone else's scrutiny. "Your brother returned something he thinks belongs to me."

"Was that all?"

"What more could there be?"

"How is one to know with brothers? They are so vexatingly closemouthed, never letting one know what is going on inside their heads."

Cordia walked over and sat down in the barber's chair, for all the world as if she meant to visit for a time. "I thought, perhaps, he had come to inform us that he had decided to stay in town for a few days. The house in Cavendish Square is just sitting there empty; a shame not to use it. One might suppose his old friends would try what they could to persuade him to linger more than just one night." She studied a minuscule imperfection in the lace bordering the sleeve of her dress. "He voiced nothing of that nature to you?"

"To me? No. What made you think he might?"

"Oh, nothing. I merely wondered, that is all. Lay it to sisterly curiosity." The lace was given further consideration. "It was just that he spoke with you at much greater length than with Mrs. Pruett and me, and I wondered if he had mentioned anything of interest."

"How can I know," Emaline said, "what a sister would find of interest regarding her brother?"

"I, or any sister for that matter, would like to know if her brother had formulated plans to take a lady to the opera, or to a play, or to something equally entertaining."

A lady? Just thinking of Liam escorting someone about town gave Emaline a sick feeling in her stomach. "He . . . he did not mention anything of that nature."

Cordia muttered something that sounded like, "Cloth-head," but Emaline could not be sure she had heard correctly.

"It stands to reason that you would want your brother to become interested in a young lady, and . . . and eventually to marry, for it must be quite lonely for you at Whitcomb Hall without any other females to talk to."

"I am lonely on occasion, that is true. But I would forego my need for conversation for the next twenty years rather than see Liam shackled to the wrong sort."

"The wrong sort?" *Naturally, Lord Seymour's sister would wish him to look as high as he dare for a wife.*

"Yes. You know what I mean. Just anybody would not do for my brother. He needs someone very special. For example, she must have a sense of humor. That is *de rigueur*. She should also be an educated lady. And in this instance I do not refer to one whose training is limited to conversing in French and playing upon the pianoforte, for Liam is an intelligent man and would not be happy with some pretty widgeon. Also, because of what he endured in the war, and the changes it wrought in him, he needs someone with compassion—one who would share his quite serious concerns for the needy veterans and their families. Finally, she should be a lady whose interests are not concentrated upon idle pleasures and hedonistic pursuits, yet one who has a joy for life and a heart capable of loving and being loved in return."

Having completed her rather staggering catalog of requirements, Cordia looked at Emaline almost as if expectant of some response. When Emaline said nothing, Cordia sighed, for all the world as though she were put out of countenance. "Have you no opinions on the subject? Nothing? Not even one suggestion as to who would make my brother a suitable wife?"

For her part, Emaline found the topic painful in the extreme. So much so that her throat tightened as though with unshed tears. "I would not presume to make suggestions about something as important as your brother's happiness."

"None whatsoever?"

Emaline could only shake her head.

"You might at least give me your thoughts on the advisability of my dropping a hint in a lady's ear, should I suspect that Liam felt a preference for her. If the lady and I were close, if she were a particular friend of mine, what think you of my suggesting to her that she let him know her true feelings?"

A friend? Thus far, the only marriageable friend Cordia had made in London was Mary Beauchamp. Had she and Mary been discussing Lady Phoebe's hope of joining the two families?

Emaline felt as though a large stone had taken up residence inside her chest. Tears stung her eyes and she turned her face away from the light, lest Cordia see the effect her words had had upon her. When she spoke, her voice sounded strained to her own ears. "It is never a good idea to meddle. If Li—if your brother forms a preference for some young lady, he will know when the time is right to declare himself."

Sighing again, Cordia rose and walked over to the door. "I will take your advice," she said. "As much as I should like to lend a hand, I believe I shall leave it all to Liam and to his lady . . . whoever she may be."

His lady. The phrase kept repeating itself in Emaline's ears. Even after Cordia wished her a good night and closed the chamber door, Emaline could still hear the words.

Cordia had as good as admitted that she wished her friend to be her sister-in-law. But what of Liam? He had not even met Mary; he might find her not to his taste. As a matter of fact, wife hunting might not be in his thoughts at all. If he had said nothing to his sister of wishing to pursue a particular lady, perhaps there was no one special at the moment.

That thought eased the pressure inside Emaline's chest. If there were no one special in Liam's life, then perhaps she— No. No. Such hopes must surely lead to heartache. Liam could have his pick of any of the young ladies at Almack's, and though Emaline was honest enough to admit that she wished she might be that one, she was not so foolish as to believe it would happen. Only in fairy tales did the handsome prince marry the penniless maiden.

But—and this *but* cheered her more than she would have thought possible—if there were no one Liam wished to pursue, what was to keep her from pursuing him?

A flirtation was not out of the question. She had managed to attract Geoffrey Beauchamp's attention by flirting, and if it worked on a rogue like Champ, it should work on Liam. There was certainly no harm in trying.

Of course, she would not be greedy in her expectations. Marriage was out of the question; no one had to tell her that. Nor would Emaline deceive herself into thinking she could make Liam wish to offer for her.

Marriage was the entire cake, and she asked for but a slice. Just a taste of the sweetness. Her wishes were simple: to be allowed to enjoy Liam's company and to laugh with him as she had done tonight. And, if she could kindle in him the kind of spark he ignited in her, she wanted a kiss. A real kiss. The kind a man gave to the woman he loved.

Ever since their journey to London, when she had awakened in his arms, she had begun to suspect that she would never know passion with anyone save Liam. Each time she saw him, she became more convinced of that fact.

When Lady Phoebe had laid out her plans for a marriage between Liam and Mary, those plans had torn at Emaline's heart like the talons of a bird of prey. Only then did she realize that she loved him. Never mind that he had no such feelings for her. Liam was the only man she would ever love. To no other man's arms would she surrender her heart, and to no other man's lips would she offer her soul. Not now. Not ever.

Only to Liam.

Yes! She would pursue him. She would not waste this opportunity.

Optimistic in the face of this decision, she threw back the covers, took the single candle over to the handsome old washstand with its Staffordshire blue and white cistern, and lit the brace of candles that stood there. Her purpose clear, she hurried to the dressing room, found the reticule that held the little book from the vitrine, and removed the volume from its hiding place.

Returning with the book to the barber's chair, Emaline made herself comfortable, tucking her bare feet beneath the hem of her plain white lawn night rail. Once again she perused the ten chapter titles of *How to Attract, Captivate, and Fascinate a Member of the Male Sex*. Hungry for knowledge, she turned to page one and began to study each line carefully. This time she would read not for the amusement of it, but for the instruction described so explicitly by Madame X.

Emaline had four weeks—no, three weeks and five days—and she meant to make the most of them. With any luck at all, that should be sufficient time to make Liam feel something for her. If not love, then at the very least, passion. When her time was up, if he showed no sign of any stronger feeling than friendship, at least she would return to Wiltshire knowing she had tried her best.

After Cordia left Emaline's bedchamber, she went belowstairs to see if the servants had returned from their half-holiday. She wished to tell Turner that she had been unable to secure the French windows in the library, for something seemed to be impeding the lock.

As she walked through the vestibule, however, she noticed the black jeweler's box Emaline had left on the ebony console, and never one to pass up an opportunity to admire something beautiful, she opened the lid.

"Ooh," she said, awed at the magnificence of the gold filigree setting and the brilliance of the dark red gems. "How absolutely splendid!" It was the work of a moment to remove the necklace and slip it around her throat.

All too aware of the lamentable fact that neither the vestibule nor the drawing room boasted a looking glass, Cordia looked about her for some shiny surface in which to view the effect of the jewelry. When no such surface presented itself, she turned to remount the stairs, her objective the glass that hung above the dressing table in her bedchamber.

Her foot had only just touched the bottom stair when she

heard the door to the kitchen rooms open at the rear of the corridor. "Turner," she called, "is that you? I am glad you have returned, for the lock on the French window will not—" She gasped.

The man who stepped into the pool of light cast by the chandelier was not the butler, but someone she had never seen before in her entire life. A large, burly man, with the pointed face of a weasel and black, angry eyes, he frightened her so badly she could not even scream.

He stopped short. Like her, he was surprised by the encounter. As the initial shock wore off, however, he stared not at her but at the stones around her neck. "Here," he said, his voice as angry as his eyes. "Where did you get that necklace?"

Chapter 10

When Cordia's blood-chilling scream finally burst forth, it did three things: It released her from her paralysis, it frightened the man into backing away from her, and it brought Emaline running to the top of the stairs.

"What is it?" Emaline asked, her voice not quite steady. "My dear, what has happened? Are you all—?" She stopped, clutching the book she held against her chest, startled to recognize the man who was only partially obscured by the shadows of the corridor.

"You!"

Vernon Brofton stepped forward, a spuriously servile smile upon his face, and made her a bow. "Beggin' your ladyship's pardon, I'm sure. Didn't mean to frighten the young lady."

"Brofton. What are you doing here?"

"In town looking for a job, I am. The new Lord Seymour seen fit to let me go, he did, and seeing as how I've known Turner and his missus for donkeys' ages, I thought I'd cadge a meal and a warm place to sleep. Didn't think anyone would mind, being as I was his lordship's valet for near eighteen years."

"I fear you are mistaken," Emaline informed him, "for I mind very much."

She had regained her composure, and though the sight of Vernon Brofton made her skin crawl, she managed to keep her voice calm and even. "Although I wish you every success in your search for employment, no one in this establishment is in need of a valet."

"I can see that, your ladyship."

He looked Cordia up and down, his appraisal slow and insulting, before returning his attention to Emaline. "Appears like there's just you and young miss in residence. Don't seem to be no men at all around the place."

His voice held a hint of glee, as though he enjoyed the idea that his words might frighten them, and Emaline was reminded of the story Hannah had related of Brofton's brutality. Adjuring herself not to let him see how terrified she was, and how badly she wanted him out of the house, she lifted her chin, using a voice that was reminiscent of Lady Phoebe at her most commanding. "Who does or does not reside here is none of your concern. The only thing you need to know is that this house belongs to me. That being so, you will oblige me by leaving the premises immediately."

Even though a staircase separated them, Emaline could see the anger darken his black eyes to pitch. "No call to turn me out, my lady. I ain't so plump in the pockets at the moment, and I could use a little—"

"No."

If she had not known of Brofton's blackmailing practices and his savage beating of poor Turner, Emaline might have been tempted to grant the man a place for the night. But she did know, and the knowledge hardened her heart. "Do not compel me to resort to the use of my father's pistol. I keep it upon my nightstand, primed and loaded, and though I should regret firing it upon one who was once employed in the house, I shall do so without remorse if you do not depart on the instant."

When the valet remained where he stood, Emaline turned and calmly strolled toward her bedchamber.

"I'm going," he yelled, his weasel's face pinched and his meaty fingers curled at his side as though he contemplated strangling her with his bare hands.

Wheeling about, he headed toward the rear of the corridor, as if to leave by way of the kitchen. Emaline stopped him. "That way," she said, pointing to the front door. "I wish to assure myself that you have truly followed my instructions."

The moment the door clicked shut behind him, Emaline snatched up the full skirt of her night rail so that she did not trip upon the hem, then hurried down the stairs and shot the bolt home.

"Come," she ordered, grabbing Cordia's hand and fairly racing along the corridor and down the stone steps to the kitchen. She did not stop until she reached the rear door and shot that bolt home as well.

Leaning against the thick, dark wood, her head back and her eyes closed, Emaline fought for breath.

"You . . . you were wonderful," Cordia said, her voice filled with awe. "So brave. So fearless."

Still struggling for air, Emaline shook her head. "Frightened beyond all reason."

"I cannot allow that to be so, not when it contradicts the testimony of my own eyes. I declare I had no notion how we were to rid ourselves of that terrifying man. But you— you knew just how it should be done. And I had no idea," she added, obviously much struck by the recollection, "that you kept a weapon beside your bed."

"A weapon? Do not be absurd."

The amazement in Cordia's face turned to puzzlement. "But you told him—that awful man—that you kept a pistol primed and loaded. You said it had belonged to your father."

"My father," Emaline explained, "never owned a pistol in his life. He was the gentlest man who ever wore the cloth. A true man of God. The most frightening item in his possession was a collection of seventeenth-century sermons from which he dearly loved to quote. They were unbelievably dull, those sermons, and I assure you, any one of them could bore a person to death."

The next day, Cordia and her maid left for the Beauchamp town house in Pall Mall scarcely five minutes before Liam arrived at Grosvenor Square. Emaline had breathed a sigh of relief when the young lady left, for she had not wanted to ruin her afternoon with Liam by telling him of Vernon Brofton's unorthodox appearance in the vestibule. She knew she would need to inform him of it sooner or later, but she and Cordia had discussed the matter at length last night and again this morning, and she was heartily sick of the subject.

She wanted to enjoy the day. Dressed in a muted yellow pelisse worn over a plain gold carriage dress—a deceptively simple costume only just arrived from Madame Julienne's—Emaline knew she looked her best, and she had no patience with anything that might spoil the moment. If she could help it, nothing was going to dampen her pleasure in the promised outing.

Five minutes after his sister's departure, Liam arrived at Seymour House. When he entered the drawing room, he found Emaline seated upon the beige brocade settee—the perfect backdrop, he decided, for both her costume and her own vibrant coloring. Looking about him and discovering that they were alone, he paused a moment, giving himself the pleasure of surveying both the ensemble and the lady wearing it.

She was beautiful. There was no other way to describe her. Though her hair was arranged in its usual unpretentious style—braided, then fastened in a figure-eight at the back of her head—the coppery tints sparkled as if with a life of their own. As well, her brown eyes displayed to advantage against the yellow of her pelisse, appearing as warm and rich as two perfectly matched gems.

Of its own accord, his appraisal ended when it reached her mouth. As his gaze lingered on her full, satiny lips—lips that glowed with the rosy pink of good health—she smiled. Unbidden, a pulse began to throb in his neck, and it was all he could do to stop himself from crossing the room and taking her into his arms. His purpose: to kiss that smile into a sigh of contentment.

Not that he would do so, of course. She was a parson's daughter, a gently reared miss just up from the country, totally unaware of how provocative she looked or how she made his blood stir in his veins. And more naive than his own sister. Devil take it, Emaline still believed in such fantasies as answered prayers and happily-ever-after.

Even knowing he should not do so, Liam continued to gaze at her, at the laughter in her eyes and the unbelievable openness and honesty in her face. Damn, but she was lovely! And he could not even tell her how beautiful she was, for well-bred ladies found all but the most innocuous compliments distasteful.

"Madam," he said, making her a bow, "you are as enchanting as you are punctual."

To his surprise, an imp of mischief lit her eyes.

"What an odd combination of compliments, sir. If I may ask, which of the two should I esteem most?"

"The latter, to be sure, ma'am, for I would not wish to be accused of offering you Spanish coin."

"As to that," she said, batting her lashes at him like some coquettish ninnyhammer, "please, offer away. I know that a lady is supposed to find compliments disagreeable, but somehow I cannot dislike them."

What May game was this? Liam felt a smile hover about his lips. He might have known it would be so, for Emaline always made him laugh. In fact, it had occurred to him only yesterday that each time he was with her, he felt a little more like his old self, like the happy young man he had been before he went off to war.

"Of course," she continued, "you need not feel obliged to *shower* admiration upon me."

His smile became a chuckle. "No?"

"Certainly not. A dozen compliments should do nicely for the moment; especially if you allocate them judiciously so that you do not neglect a single aspect of either my raiment or my manners."

"In regard to your manners," he said dryly, "a number of comments have already sprung to my mind. Though I seriously doubt you will wish to hear the lot."

The minx only just managed to hide her smile. "Lah, sir. Never tell me that my forthrightness has given you a disgust of me. If that is the case, then feel free to cut the number of compliments by half."

"Still a superfluous number, for I assure you I shall need but one."

Reaching out his hand, he assisted her to her feet, and when she was standing, he retained his hold on her so that they were but inches apart. Wishing he might do more than hold her hand, he leaned closer, his mouth very nearly brushing her ear. "You," he whispered, "are a brazen hussy."

Their second drive to Westminster Abbey was unmarred by either heavy traffic or dray accidents, and as they sped past St. James's, then finally turned in at the carriage entrance, their conversation was light and inconsequential. A circumstance, Emaline told herself, that resulted from the groom's occupation of the elevated seat up behind them. She also used the servant's presence as an excuse to postpone informing Liam of Brofton's visit, delaying the introduction of such an unpleasant topic until they returned to Seymour House.

As Liam helped her from the curricle, then led her toward the west door, he asked if she wished to join one of the guided tours. "Or will you trust your visit to me?"

When she raised her brow in question, he patted his coat, as though to reveal to her the existence of the promised guidebook. "Should you find me deficient in pertinent information, you have only to let me know, and we will join one of the groups."

"Oh, no. I put myself entirely in your hands."

"Very well," he said. "Allow me to begin by informing you that the nave we are about to enter is seventy-two feet wide and one hundred and two feet high."

Emaline's surprise at Liam's having learned this information for her edification gave way to total awe when she passed through the ancient door. Awe at the Abbey's soaring vaulting as well as the number of monuments in the transepts and aisles. To her further amazement, as they traversed through the nave en route to Poet's Corner, Liam was able to name a number of the famous sculptors responsible for the monuments.

It was not to be wondered at that in time a small group gathered, following them at a discreet distance, listening to Liam's sometime admiring, sometime acerbic remarks upon this poet or that politician immortalized in stone. Attempting to outdistance their entourage, Liam put his hand beneath Emaline's elbow and guided her to the low flight of steps that led to the sanctuary. They had paused at the steps and were admiring the tapestry hung behind the altarpiece, when a rather portly gentleman approached them.

Dressed in a buckram-filled coat of bottle green worn over an unfortunate waistcoat of gold and maroon stripes, the gentleman reminded Emaline of nothing so much as a rainbow-hued beetle. Owing to the extreme snugness of his lime green inexpressibles, he was obliged to mince rather than walk. Nonetheless, he came forward, his pudgy hand extended in greeting, confident of his welcome. "Whitcomb, old boy. Is that you?"

Muttering something beneath his breath, Liam stepped forward and took the offered hand. "Vickery."

As it transpired, the rotund gentleman was an old classmate of Liam's from Eton, and within moments he was begging leave to introduce his wife, his mother-in-law, and his wife's sister, a very young lady who was to make her bow during the little season. Liam could do nothing but acquiesce.

Any possible doubts Emaline may have had about Liam's being a *premier parti* were put to rest by the unrestrained fawning of Mrs. Vickery and her mother. Once the two women discovered that Liam was a peer, and that Emaline was not his wife but the *dowager* Lady Seymour, their sycophancy knew no bounds.

Within a matter of minutes they had all but tossed the handkerchief at him, dropping increasingly broader hints regarding the younger lady's willingness to stand up with him at Almack's, and attempting to extract from Liam a promise to attend the proposed ball marking her introduction to society. Though he steadfastly failed to catch their meaning, they were undeterred, and trying another tack, they attempted to discover his preferences regarding musicales as opposed to alfresco nuncheons.

To Emaline, the women extended no more than the barest civility, while the gentleman seemed to consider her presence at the Abbey as his reward for escorting his wife and his in-laws. His fulsome compliments annoyed her almost as much as the women's gaucherie. Sparing a moment to glance at Liam, she saw that he too wished the entire family otherwise.

"Your pardon," he said, when it began to look as if the foursome would never leave, "but I fear my cousin is fatigued." Bowing to the ladies and then to his old classmate, Liam found Emaline's hand and placed it in the crook of his arm. "If you will excuse us, I really must escort Lady Seymour back to her carriage."

"Of course," replied the mother-in-law with a sugary smile, not at all deceived by this strategem, "we older ladies tire easily. Is that not so, Lady Seymour?"

With her arm tucked snugly beneath his, Emaline could feel Liam's rib cage shake as he tried not to laugh, and only when they were out of hearing of the family party did she give herself the pleasure of telling him what she thought of his choice of little white lies.

"How dare you put me at the mercy of that harpy's tongue!"

"Your pardon," he said, the sincerity of his words belied

by the laughter in his eyes. "It was not well done of me, I know, but I knew I could trust you not to betray me."

Although Emaline felt mollified by his rationale, the female in her would not let him off the hook that easily. "It would be no more than you deserve, Liam Whitcomb, if I pretended to faint this very moment, obliging you to carry my aged person all the way to the curricle. We should just see who was tired after that exercise."

He squeezed her captured arm against his side. "Is that a dare? If so, I accept. Swoon away. I am prepared to catch you."

At the thought of being borne in Liam's arms, Emaline experienced a flush of warmth that was pleasurable in the extreme. And though she knew he spoke in jest, the image of him wrapping one strong arm around her waist, then scooping her off the ground and holding her to his chest was so enticing it left her feeling slightly weak in the knees.

It also reminded her that she had planned to do a bit of beguiling of her own.

Recalling the instructions of Madam X that one must find a way to touch the gentleman one wished to captivate, Emaline took a steadying breath, then made as if to reclaim her hand from the crook of Liam's elbow. When he loosened his hold on her, however, she did not move away. Instead, she let her fingers trail ever so slowly down the sleeve of his Devonshire brown coat until they encountered the hard warmth of the heel of his hand.

When she had imagined this move, she had envisioned Liam responding to her. Smiling, joking, teasing . . . something! He did none of those things. Aside from a slight rigidness about his jaw, he seemed not to notice her actions. He looked to neither right nor left, and if he even remembered that she was there, he gave no sign of it.

Hesitating only a moment, she moistened her suddenly dry lips then eased the pads of her fingers across Liam's open palm, not stopping until she reached the ends of his fingers. His hand was firm and faintly callused, and though he made no attempt to capture her fingers, she knew that if he had, she would have felt a strong, masterful grasp.

With her hand against his, her nervousness disappeared, replaced by a lovely tingling sensation that seemed to be traveling up her spine. In no hurry to end the contact, she drew her fingertips back up from his, enjoying the almost involuntary curving of his palm as she skimmed that area once again. She tried to will him to take her hand. He did not.

When she found her progress momentarily thwarted by the sleeve of his shirt, Emaline obeyed her instincts and slipped her fingers beneath the snug, linen band. To her surprise, the moment she touched the engorged veins of Liam's thick, powerful wrist, she became so aware of his masculinity and her answering femininity that a shock wave washed over her, nearly paralyzing her in its intensity.

Unprepared for such a primal reaction, not to mention the accompanying frisson of fear, Emaline's audacity deserted her. Instantly she snatched her arm away. Feeling unexplainably vulnerable, she hurried her footsteps, walking slightly ahead of him. For the last few feet of the nave she saw nothing; the delicate carvings on screens and arches were all but ignored. She prayed the blush that crept up her face went equally unnoticed.

Her plan had gone awry. For one thing, she had not been prepared for the lack of response from Liam. Especially not when she had found touching him an even headier experience than she had imagined. And she had certainly not bargained for the heart-stopping excitement that had surged through her when she slipped her fingers beneath his shirt and felt his wrist.

She tried to walk faster, but he caught up with her, and in an instant she felt his left arm stretch beyond her shoulder to push open the heavy wooden door. Unable to stop herself, she stared at the strong wrist whose contours her fingers knew so intimately. "Here," he said, placing his hand at the small of her back, "allow me."

Through the various layers of her pelisse, her dress, her petticoat, her stays, and her shift, Emaline felt the heat of Liam's skin as it touched hers, and the sensation sent her floating above the Abbey floor. *Allow him?* She was tempted to beg him.

"Careful," he said, gently nudging her across the threshold, "watch your footing on that last step."

His prosiac words brought her crashing back to earth. He had touched her only to assist her out the door. She felt as though someone had doused her with a bucket of cold brook water. Obviously her touch had not affected him in the same way his had affected her.

Feeling like the veryest fool, she prayed the earth would open up and swallow her. So much for Madame X's instructions. Emaline had done just as the author said, and Liam had not been the least bit attracted. As for his being captivated or fascinated, she would count herself fortunate if she had not given him a thorough disgust of her!

Spying the curricle, she did not wait for Liam to signal the groom, but hurried across the gravel drive toward the carriage, wishing with all her heart that she need not sit next to Liam for the full twenty-minute drive back to Grosvenor Square. Crawling the entire distance on her hands and knees seemed infinitely preferable.

"I am sorry," he said, very close to her ear.

She stiffened. "I am sure I do not know what you mean." If he meant to talk about her indiscretion, she would never be able to endure it.

"I apologize for having rushed you through the Abbey. I would promise to bring you back again, but I cannot think you would believe me a third time. In fact," he said, taking her elbow and helping her into the curricle, "I would not blame you if you refused out of hand my invitation to escort you and Cordia to Vauxhall Gardens this evening."

Chapter 11

"Are you ready?" Cordia called from the other side of the bedchamber door. "Has the magic been wrought? I vow I can hardly wait to view the outcome of such a secretive conspiracy."

"Come in, then, and see for yourself."

Hannah stepped aside and Emaline rose from the little stool the maid had pulled up to the looking glass. Squaring her shoulders and lifting her chin, she turned to face the door so that she could read Cordia's initial reaction. First impressions being the truest, if the young lady so much as blinked, Emaline had every intention of returning to the looking glass and obliterating the rather fanciful coiffure Hannah had worked with such tender care. She would brush out every last curl, then braid her thick hair and fashion it in its usual figure-eight.

"Oh, Emaline!" Cordia said from the doorway, her eyes wide. "You look so . . . so . . ."

When she said nothing more, Emaline reached her hand up rather self-consciously to her almost-bare shoulder, where a single curl rested. The lone tress had been allowed to tumble free, while the remainder of her coppery curls had been lifted up and back so they cascaded cunningly from the crown of her head to the nape of her neck. "You approve?"

The young lady kissed her fingers in a Gallic gesture that was all the rage. "You are *très ravissante.*"

"You do not think I look . . . foolish?"

"Of course you do not! Whatever put such an idea into your head?"

Emaline sighed. "Curls. At my age. A woman of seven and twenty should probably be wearing a cap."

"Pshaw," Cordia said, rejecting the argument. "Seven and twenty might be old for a single woman, but for a widow, it is considered quite young. Everyone will think you very dashing."

Reassured, Emaline turned back to the glass for one last look at the midnight-blue evening dress, with its rather low neckline and its bouffant sleeves.

"Her ladyship's a treat for the eyes, right enough," Hannah added, busying herself with clearing the Beau Brummel of the remaining hairpins. "All she needs is a bit of jewelry. 'Twould finish the dress off to a nicety."

Touching her exposed collarbone, Emaline said, "I have my gold brooch, but I do not think it quite fancy enough for this silk faille. What say you, Cordia?"

After looking Emaline up and down, the young lady suddenly snapped her fingers. "I have it. I know what would be perfect. The ruby necklace."

"Oh, but I—"

Stepping over to the Beau Brummel, the determined miss took the pins from Hannah's hands and told her to run down to the kitchen and see if she could find a black leather jeweler's box.

"In the kitchen, miss?"

"Yes, I . . . er, left it there last night when I went in search of . . . a glass of milk."

As soon as the door closed behind the maid, Emaline breathed a sigh of relief. "You were very quick, my dear."

Cordia shook her head. "Me and my mouth. After you telling me specifically that you did not wish the servants frightened unnecessarily, I almost let the cat out of the bag. I came that close to telling Hannah about the valet being here."

"But you did not, so all is well. Now there is no reason why she or the Turners should ever have to know anything about it. Brofton is gone, and there's an end to it. We need never think of him again."

Liam had only just handed his hat to the butler when he heard footsteps on the stairs. Glancing upward expectantly, he saw his sister descending the steps, charmingly attired in a gown of palest rose sarcenet over a white slip. With her dusky curls pulled into a loose knot at the top of her head, and the knot circled with a string of tiny pearls, she looked surprisingly grown-up.

On the verge of complimenting Cordia upon her looks, he looked just behind her, spying Emaline. Instantly, all thoughts of his sister vanished from his consciousness. He had eyes for none save the lady in blue.

"You are prompt as usual," Cordia said, reaching up to give him a quick buss on the cheek. "Shall I ask Turner to fetch you a glass of sherry before we leave?"

Liam shook his head. He had no need for strong spirits; a man could become intoxicated just looking at Emaline. The gown she wore exposed her softly sloping shoulders and fit her lovely figure to perfection. While the color of the material—the dark blue of an autumn sky in those breathless moments just before the sun chases away the night—was magic against her clear, satiny skin. In addition, the paste necklace, with her beautiful throat as its foil, appeared to be set with gems of inestimable value.

"What say you?" Cordia asked, reminding him that he and Emaline were not alone in the vestibule. "Will we shame you before your friends?"

Returning his attention to his irrepressible sister, he watched her do a pirouette, displaying her new finery. "I think it more likely, little one, that I shall lament not having availed myself of one of those canes with a concealed sword. It goes without saying that I shall be obliged to fight off scores of admirers this evening, for you look fine as five-pence."

Cordia inclined her head in acknowledgement of the brotherly praise, then spoiled the regal effect by giggling. "But what of Emaline?" she asked. "Does she not look pretty as well?"

"No," he said, taking the blue swansdown wrap Emaline carried over her arm and placing it around her shoulders. "Lady Seymour looks unbelievably beautiful."

Rather than go by water, they traveled to Vauxhall Gardens via Westminster Bridge, and by the time Liam handed the ladies out of the berline, a million stars bejeweled the sky, and a full moon cast its yellow-white glow upon the earth.

Adding to nature's illumination, the arbors and walks of the pleasure garden were hung with thousands of colorful lanterns. "A necessity," Liam informed Emaline when she commented upon the surprising amount of light, "for as the gardens and the firework displays have grown more popular, knavery has increased."

Knaves notwithstanding, Emaline wished to be nowhere else in the world than here with Liam. Breathing a sigh of pure contentment, she looked around her. Vauxhall was like a fairyland, and she was Cinderella at the ball, and Liam a Prince Charming worthy of the name. A prince to steal any woman's heart.

Unbelievably beautiful, he had said.

Once, in every woman's life, she should have those words spoken to her. They were like heavenly music, uplifting to the soul, and Emaline's heart still sang at the memory. It was a memory made more exquisite by the knowledge that the words were spoken from the heart, and not because they had been prompted by artifice or clever stratagem on her part.

Vowing to send Madame X's little book of tricks back to Wiltshire on the morrow, Emaline gave herself up to the pleasures to be found at the famous garden.

"Knavery?" Cordia said, her voice sounding more intrigued than frightened.

"Yes. But you need have no fear of uninvited attention," Liam assured his sister, offering his right arm to her and his left to Emaline. "Not as long as you follow two basic rules. The first: Stay with your party. The second: Avoid the infamous Dark Walk, no matter who offers to escort you there."

"Since you are our sole escort for the evening," Cordia said with a suspicious meekness, "we can promise you that we will not go anyplace you would not like. As for any subsequent times we might come here," she added, leaning around her brother to give Emaline a wink, "who can say?"

"Impertinent chit!" Liam said.

In very good spirits with one another, the three of them strolled the Grand Walk, headed toward the Grove and the supper box Liam had reserved for the evening. Set back from the walk, and surrounded by a railing for added privacy, the box was close enough to the orchestra to hear the music, but not so near that conversation was made impossible. After they were seated around the table, with its crisp linen cloth and its centerpiece of small topiary, charmingly threaded through with silky white clematis, the box was declared by Cordia to be *ne plus ultra."*

"You are become quite *French,"* her brother remarked, an indulgent smile upon his lips. "I can see how it will be by the season's end. You will have acquired so much town bronze that I will be obliged—"

Whatever he had meant to say, the words were forgotten as two elegantly attired gentlemen approached the box. Stopping just on the other side of the rail, the twosome made their bows.

"Seymour," a gentleman of about three and twenty said politely.

"Liam, old son!" the other said, a roguish smile lighting his gray eyes. "Fancy meeting you here. I was just saying to Fitz, 'Who is that lucky devil escorting the two most beautiful ladies in London?' Then, of course, I realized that I cared not who the escort was, but only what I need do to steal the ladies away from him."

"Champ," Liam said, bowing rather reservedly to his old friend. Then, "Good evening, Fitzhugh. Allow me to make you known to Lady Seymour and my sister."

Emaline noted that although Liam was unfailingly polite to the visitors, the smile he had worn earlier had definitely disappeared. The same could not be said for his sister, however. The sudden brilliance in that young lady's eyes was enough to blind the unwary.

"How do you do, Mr. Fitzhugh," Cordia said. Then turning to Champ, "And how are your sister and Lady Phoebe this evening?"

"They are well, Miss Cordia. Thank you for asking."

That Champ's reply was innocent of his usual easy gallantry spoke volumes to Emaline. It would appear that the gentleman was as smitten by the young lady as she was by him, and that for all his skill at flirtation, he was experiencing the usual insecurities of a man on his way to being in love.

It was not to be expected that Liam would immediately discern the truth of the situation, since an unrelated gentleman's admiration for one's sister always comes as a complete surprise to the brother, never mind how much he may hold her in esteem himself. Therefore, Liam paid little heed to what *did not* pass between his sister and his friend, watching instead the flirtatious banter exchanged by his friend and Emaline.

"I see we are intruding," Champ said when the waiter came to take the dinner order. "And Liam will be wishing Fitz and me on a slow packet to India."

"Packets to India notwithstanding," Liam replied, "if that is a hint for me to be so good as to include you two bachelors in my party, allow me to inform you that I have seen you employ such tactics for years, and I am not such a flat as to be taken in by them. Find your own ladies."

Emaline very nearly gasped, for Liam's reply bordered on a snub.

Fortunately, Champ took no offense, merely laughing at his old friend. "Acquit me, old son, for I am with a party myself." He motioned toward a supper box a small distance away, and as one his audience turned to look.

Seated at that table was an elderly gentleman of distinguished bearing, and two ladies. The younger of the two lifted her hand shyy, waving at Emaline and Cordia, while the older lady, her back ramrod straight as though she were a queen, did not so much as nod.

"It is Mary," Cordia said. "And . . . and Lady Phoebe. Shall we go over?"

"Let us postpone the pleasure until later," Emaline replied, "for I believe the waiter is ready to serve their dinner." Glad of the excuse, Emaline breathed a sigh of relief, for she discerned Lady Phoebe's disapproval even from a distance. The cause of that censure was not difficult to assess. Having already chosen Liam as her future son-in-law, her ladyship probably considered Emaline to be poaching on private preserves, and only when Liam rose and made a bow in their direction did the lady thaw enough to vouchsafe a slight smile.

Mr. Fitzhugh poked his elbow in Champ's ribs. "Like my mutton hot, don't you know."

"Of course," Champ replied, "we should be going." Then, with rare formality, he turned to Liam. "Since my party is one lady shy and yours is one gentleman shy, may I return later to help you escort your ladies to the firework presentation?"

Hints might be ignored, but a direct question could not be disregarded. After all, this was Liam's oldest friend. "We shall await your return," he said.

For a pair of ladies unjaded by an excess of town entertainments, the dinner was everything they could have asked. And only after the famous shaved ham had been devoured, and Cordia had been allowed her first glass of champagne, did they begin to speak of the delights in store for them at the firework display.

THE RUBY NECKLACE

"I have heard," Cordia said, "that the tableaux are quite something to behold, and that they take months to stage."

"That is true," Liam replied, "though do not expect anything so spectacular as last year's Sea Battle Enactment, with its cannon fire and burning ship."

The young lady's eyes grew wide with wonder. "Oh, Liam. I should have loved to see that. Do you know the theme of the current presentation?"

Her brother failed to reply to her question, for having spied his friend approaching their box at a quick pace, Liam very nearly turned over his chair in his haste to rise and offer Emaline his arm. "Do you mind," he asked, looking over his shoulder at his sister, "favoring Champ with your company?"

Sparing no time to listen to Cordia's response, nor to notice the blushes that colored her cheeks, Liam hurried Emaline down the steps before the gentleman arrived. Within minutes the couple had joined the steady stream of people headed down the gravel path to the display. Cordia and Champ, along with Mr. Fitzhugh and Miss Mary Beauchamp, found places some distance behind them.

During the firework exhibit, conversation was impossible. Nothing could be heard above the cacophony of thousands of whistling, hissing, and exploding rockets, save the collective "oohs" and "ahs" of the crowd. Only after the finale, when the last of the sparkling reds, blues, greens, and yellows had cascaded magically from the sky to land with an anticlimactic fizzle upon the waters of the lake and on the ground, was Liam able to hear Emaline's full impression of what she had seen.

They had strolled some distance up the gravel walk and stopped to sit upon a wooden bench encircling a sturdy elm tree when he asked, "Well, ma'am, what think you?"

"It takes one's breath away," she said, still awed by the unbelievably sophisticated exhibition. "The sheer splendor of it. The patterns. The colors."

"The noise," he interjected.

"That, too," she said, pressing her fingers to her ears as though the sounds were still echoing inside her head. "It occurs to me that I should warn you, sir, if you know the secrets of the universe and were wishful of disclosing them to me, now is not the best time. At the moment, anything below a shout is beyond my capabilities."

Because Liam was such a jokester, Emaline was not surprised when he spoke again, moving his mouth without voicing the words, as if to make her think she had lost her hearing. It was only after she had begun to laugh that she realized what he was pretending to say. Or, rather, what she thought he was pretending to say.

"The moon," his soundless lips declared, *"has cast its magic upon your face, leaving your eyes sparkling with its light. And I would taste the shimmering touch of heaven upon your lips."*

Speechless herself, Emaline looked up at him, willing him to repeat what he had just said—to say it aloud. Only then would she know how to respond.

A taste of heaven? Had he really said that?

She was shocked. Surprised. Breathless. Unable to think of a proper response, yet knowing with all her heart what she would like to do, if they were not in the midst of such a throng.

"Liam, I—"

"Lord love us," said a female who paused quite close by, her bright green silk taffeta gown with its pink and yellow stripes all but glowing in the lantern light, "you would have thought I'd seen enough of these displays to remember to cover my ears." She waggled her finger at her burly companion. "If I'm deaf as a post before I'm much older, Johnny Barham, I will know where to lay the blame."

The unrepentant fellow gave her a squeeze around the waist. "You can lay anything you like against me," he said suggestively.

"Naughty boy," the woman said with a giggle, pushing him away. "I'll thank you to remember where we are. After all, I've got me standards."

Emaline looked away from the couple, returning her gaze to Liam, wishing she understood the message in those unreadable blue eyes. She too must remember where they were—in a public place, with hundreds of onlookers. But even if they had been alone, what she longed to do, which was to throw herself into Liam's arms and offer him her moonlit lips, was out of the question.

Like the female in green, she had her standards.

Before Emaline threw herself into a man's arms, and kissed him with all the passion and abandon her heart cried out to give, she ought at least to wait until she was certain the man had said he wanted her to do so.

She only *thought* Liam had said he wished to kiss her. What if he had not? And what if she had obeyed her impulse and thrown herself at him?

Feeling embarrassed because of what she wanted to do, and despondent that her feelings were not reciprocated, she gave her attention to the couple.

There was something vaguely familiar about the woman who had spoken. Though Emaline was acquainted with almost no one in London, the hair beneath the green turban with its curling, gold feather seemed so familiar. Orange. There was no other word for it. Only one other time had she seen hair that color; it was in the drawing room at Ambrose's estate, and the owner of the hair had been the original choice for Lady Seymour.

Lifting her hand, Emaline called out, "Excuse me."

The thick-set man turned first, removing his curly beaver when he saw who had spoken. "Yes, miss?"

"Well, lah," said the woman, her face wreathed in smiles, "if it ain't Lady Seymour. And his lordship."

Emaline smiled, glad to have something other than Liam's whispered words to think about. "Agnes," she said. "Hello."

Chapter 12

Though Liam was unfailingly polite, it was obvious that both he and Johnny Barham were uncomfortable with the meeting. Sensing that she might have committed a faux pas by acknowledging the acquaintance in so public a place, Emaline did little more than exchange remarks with Agnes regarding the beauty of the garden and the wonders of the firework display. "I shall be returning to Wiltshire soon," she said after a few more pleasantries, "but perhaps we shall meet again."

"And if we don't," Agnes said in parting, "here's luck to you, your ladyship."

Agnes and Johnny hurried away, leaving Liam and Emaline to stroll at a more leisurely pace back to the rented box. While they walked, Liam remained curiously quiet, almost as if he had been posed a riddle whose solution he found much too complex to rush.

Emaline refrained from speech as well. Suspecting that he might feel it incumbent upon him to give her a hint about the social blindness that ladies were expected to affect when confronted with women of easy virtue, she was surprised when he finally spoke.

"You are a credit to your father's teachings," he said. "And though I have been used to thinking that I ought not to have coerced you into marrying my cousin, I begin to think it was the wisest thing I ever did."

"Wisest?" she said, puzzlement in her voice, "for whom?"

"The answer to that question," he replied, taking her hand and placing it in the crook of his arm, "must, for the moment, remain one of those unwhispered secrets of the universe."

The trip back to Seymour House was completed in almost total silence, a circumstance that suited Emaline to a nicety, for she was in no frame of mind to utter polite inanities for a half hour. Too much was going on inside her head. There were too many questions and too few answers. She was still uncertain about that scene in the moonlight. One moment she was convinced she had misread the whole, then the next minute, after picturing Liam's moving lips once again, she was equally convinced he had said he wanted to kiss her.

If that were true, then why did he not tell her so? Or just do it! It was not as if she were some naive chit just out of the schoolroom. Had she not shown him in every way possible that she wanted his kiss?

She was no closer to solving the riddle when the berline turned onto Brook Street and stopped at the curb before the town house. Nor did it lessen her confusion when, just outside the entrance door, Liam lifted her hand to his lips for the briefest of salutes, thanking her politely for giving him the pleasure of her company.

"We shall meet again," he said.

Emaline had only just begun to feel confident when he threw her into confusion by adding, "Just as soon as I return."

"Return? Where are you g—?" She stopped, realizing how close she had come to betraying how much she cared. "Forgive me. I have no right to question your comings and goings."

"Not now, perhaps," he said softly, making even more of a jumble of her disordered nerves.

Giving her hand a squeeze, he begged her pardon for teasing her. "I must return to Whitcomb Hall for a day or so. Business decisions require my attention."

"Of course," she said, trying for a blasé tone.

When she would have turned to enter the house, he did not release her hand, but gave it a gentle tug, obliging her to look at him once again.

"You are very beautiful," he whispered. Then he lifted her captured hand and pressed the pad of her forefinger against his lips, holding it a willing captive.

Their gazes met. Cool blue losing itself in warm brown. For a breathless moment—an eternity—they stared at each other, and Emaline felt her entire being ignite with longing. As though of its own accord, her body swayed toward him, obeying an instinct as old as time.

Before time could have its way, however, Liam stepped back, putting several feet of space between them. When he spoke, his voice was strained, almost harsh. "You give so freely," he said, "and it would be so easy for me to take. So, so easy."

Without explaining, he turned and hurried to the waiting coach, slamming the door behind him and virtually disappearing into the darkness inside the vehicle. Within seconds, the coachman gave the horses their office and the berline sped away into the night.

Still reeling, as much from the reaction of her body to

Liam's slightest touch as to his parting words, Emaline went inside the house and closed the door behind her.

Since Turner was nowhere in sight, she shot the bolt, took up the candle left for her on the ebony console, then climbed the stairs to her bedchamber. She had only just opened the door when she stopped, aghast at the startling disorder of the room. Drawers were dumped onto the floor, newly arrived bandboxes were opened and tossed aside, and the mattress lay half off the bed, its ticking ripped from top to bottom and the stuffing thrown everywhere.

An instant later, still trying to convince herself that this was a trick of her eyes, she heard Cordia scream.

With her knees knocking and her hand trembling so badly she very nearly extinguished the light from the single candle, Emaline ran to the front bedchamber. That room, like her own, was in total disarray. It was also in total darkness, with no sign of its inhabiter.

Her heart in her throat, Emaline yelled, "Cordia! Where are you?"

"Here," came the frightened reply.

Turning with relief at the sound of the girl's voice, she discovered her peering from around the turn of the stairs, at the next landing up.

"Come," Cordia said, the request a quaking whisper, "it is Mrs. Pruett."

Lifting the hem of her skirt, Emaline hurried up the stairs to the garden-facing room occupied by the chaperone. Cordia's candle lay on the floor just outside the door, but a brace of work candles was lit on the rosewood pouch-table beside the chaperone's preferred slipper chair, revealing the lady herself.

Mrs. Pruett sat upright in her chair, her injured leg propped on a tufted hassock, very much as she had been when Emaline bid her good evening before leaving for Vauxhall Gardens. Only this time, the elderly lady's hands were no longer occupied with the darning of a pair of still-serviceable cotton stockings; they were tied behind her back, and her mouth was cruelly bound by the mended hosiery. At her right temple, peeking from beneath her gray fringe, a large bump already showed signs of discoloration.

Emaline set her candle down on the bedside table just inside the room and rushed to the lady's rescue. After untying Mrs. Pruett's mouth, she set about releasing her hands, then caught the woman as she slumped forward, bidding Cordia search for the chaperone's *sal volatile*. "For it is not to be wondered at that she has swooned," Emaline explained, "Though I wish she had not, for I must know who did this dreadful deed. And when."

It was a full ten minutes before Emaline's questions could be answered. And even then, she could only guess at the villain's identity, for the man had been as surprised to discover Mrs. Pruett in occupancy of the room as the lady was to discover a stranger opening her bedchamber door.

"At first, I had thought it must be Hannah come to help me to bed," she told them, "though I wondered at her so forgetting herself as to enter the room without knocking and waiting to be granted access. When I saw it was not the maid, but a man, I screamed. That is when he rushed at me, dealing me a blow that rendered me senseless for a time. When I was myself again, the chamber was empty and in the regrettable state you see before you."

Like the rooms below, this one had been ruthlessly overturned. Giving the chaos only a cursory glance, Emaline asked Mrs. Pruett if she could describe the man.

"Youngish," she said.

Cordia and Emaline exchanged knowing glances. For a

woman of Mrs. Pruett's years, any age below fifty was considered youngish. "Can you give me a slightly more pertinent description, ma'am?"

"I recall that he was quite sinister looking, with black, malevolent eyes, and his face had the look of an animal of some sort."

"A weasel?" Emaline asked, anger fairly choking her as she began to suspect the villain's identity.

"Why, yes. The very animal. What a coincidence that you should guess correctly on the first try."

"Coincidence played no part in my naming of the animal, ma'am, just as it will play no part in my naming of the man. It can be none other than Vernon Brofton, my late husband's valet."

She turned her face away from the elderly lady's startled gaze. "I only pray you can find it in your heart to forgive me, ma'am, for this unfortunate incident is entirely my fault."

Cordia would not allow Emaline to shoulder the complete blame for not telling anyone about Brofton's earlier break-in. "For I, too, have a voice. I could have mentioned it to my brother, had I not been more interested in the drape of my new dress and the arrangement of my hair."

"I agree with Cordia," Mrs. Pruett added. "You must not be so hard on yourself, Lady Seymour. How could you know the man would return? It was enough that you told Turner to be on the watch for—." She paused, obviously detecting Emaline's sudden concern. "Surely you told the butler! Not to do so would be foolish beyond permission. Such disregard for the consequences would be inexcus—"

Emaline waved aside Mrs. Pruett's comments, her concern turned to very real fear, for Brofton had a history of violence. "Cordia? You entered the house first. Did Turner open the door for you?"

"Why, no. The door was ajar. My thoughts were otherwhere, and when I did not see anyone, I supposed Turner had merely stepped away for the moment. You do not think—"

"Stay here," she instructed, taking up her candle. "And lock the door behind me."

Not waiting to hear the remainder of Mrs. Pruett's impassioned plea for her to stay locked in with them until morning, Emaline made her way back down the stairs, wishing the silk of her dress did not *swish* so loudly, and that her papa truly had owned a pistol.

At the vestibule, she paused only long enough to take a deep breath, then she tiptoed to the rear of the corridor until she came to the door leading to the kitchen rooms. Placing her ear to the heavy wooden panel, she listened for several minutes. Hearing nothing but the incessant gnawing of a mouse in the wall, she eased the door open and slowly descended the six stone steps that gave onto the lowest level of the house.

A lamp burned in the center of the scrubbed deal table, and four places were set with plates and cups. The halfeaten meals on the plates, as well as the almost-full cups of coffee, attested to the fact that the four servants had been in the middle of their dinner when they were interrupted by something—or someone.

But where were they now?

The service entrance was bolted from the inside, so whoever was here had not gone out that way. Feeling more frightened by the minute, Emaline turned to leave, and as she did so, she thought she heard something within the larder. Another mouse? She waited for a full minute, not moving, not even daring to breathe, and finally the sound came again. If that were a mouse, she hoped she never met it face to face, for from the noise it made, the animal must weigh at least ten stone.

When the handle to the larder door shook furiously, Emaline very nearly jumped out of her skin. "Who . . . who is there?" she called.

The sudden frenzy of yells and pleas for help sent Emaline running to the larder, which had a large iron key protruding from its lock. After she turned the key, the door was shoved open and she was very nearly trampled as four grateful prisoners rushed to freedom.

"We ought to have told you about Brofton, my lady."

"Turner's right," seconded his wife. "But we were frightened for our positions. Too many people out of work these days, and where there is a position to be had, they seldom want both a butler and a housekeeper." She lifted her apron to suddenly damp eyes. "I would die without I could be with Georgie every day."

Turner cleared his throat then patted his wife's shoulder, mortified to be exhibiting such personal emotion before the others. "Stubble it, Fanny, there's a good girl. We aren't sacked yet."

The five of them sat at the deal table, fresh coffee poured all around, their shared fear having pushed aside, for the moment at least, the barrier that separated employer from employee.

Emaline sipped the strong brew, feeling its reviving warmth trickle down her throat to warm her inside. "All of us have things we wish we had done or said before the time ran out. What we need to do now is decide what is best to be done."

"Can we not just forget it, your ladyship?"

She shook her head. "I fear not, Mrs. Turner. For one thing, Mrs. Pruett has sustained an injury and will probably wish to lodge a complaint. But even if that were not so, what is to keep Brofton from breaking in here a third time? You say he forced you into the larder using a pistol. What is to prevent him from returning with an entire gang of cutthroats, each of them brandishing pistols? Another time, a bump on the head might not be the only injury."

"Perhaps he got what he was looking for," Hannah offered hopefully.

"If what I suspect is true," Emaline said, "he did not."

She touched the necklace at her throat, feeling the delicate gold filigree and letting her fingers progress down the row of dark red gems until they ended at the large teardrop suspended from the center. All the while, she looked at the butler. "What think you, Turner?"

" 'Twas Georgie's brother's doing!" the housekeeper interjected. She stared at the necklace, her eyes wide with fear, as though it were a deadly serpent. "Always a wild one, was Samuel. My Georgie didn't know nothing about it until after the fact."

"I have no doubt of that," Emaline assured her. "However, if it is the necklace Brofton wanted, as you can see, he did not get it. That being true, I believe he will return."

The butler hid his face in his hands, his shoulders bent in defeat. "He'll be back, my lady. I'd stake my life on that."

"You might well," she replied.

He looked up sharply, as though seeing her for the first time. "You have to understand about my brother. He was always a wild nipper, sure enough. Up for every lark. But before he took up with Vernon Brofton, his transgressions were little more than boyish pranks. It was Brofton who talked him into helping rob Mr. Edgar Whitcomb."

Turner leaned forward, as if to stress the importance of his remarks. "Brofton has a demon in him, and he doesn't reason like a normal man. He blames Samuel for having the stolen gems in his hands when he was shot. Says Samuel lost *his* rubies, and now we—Fanny and me—owe him. He thinks the necklace belongs to him simply because he went after it, and he believes he has a right to retrieve what is his."

Shuddering at the thought of being pursued by the unbalanced Brofton, Emaline was tempted to yank the necklace from her throat and fling it across the room, leaving it on the stone floor where the valet could find it. But, of course, she knew that would not serve. The moment he discovered the gems were paste, he would come back, angrier than ever, perhaps to wreak his vengeance upon all those in the house.

"We cannot ignore this threat," she said.

"No, my lady," Turner said. "But other than securing the house, what are we to do?"

Emaline knew exactly what she wanted to do, and had not the least doubt as to what—or who—was needed to make her feel safe again. "I shall send a note around to Cavendish Square. Lord Seymour will know how to handle this matter."

Unaware of the drama being enacted in Grosvenor Square, Liam returned to the rented town house in Cavendish Square to find everything in readiness for his early departure for Surrey the next day. The trip was important, for he was to make a formal presentation of the land, and announce his plans for the construction of the new Benevolent Institution. In all honesty, though, he wished he did not have to leave London at this particular time.

"You want I should 'elp you disrobe, Major?" Felix Harvey asked, setting a jug of hot water on the marble top wash stand. The homely face was alight with curiosity.

"No. Go on to bed. We've a busy day tomorrow."

Not so easily put off, the valet stood his ground, looking about the room as if searching for some task left undone. "And what of this evening, sir? Did Miss enjoy 'er first night out on the town?"

"She seemed to."

"And 'er ladyship?" he asked nonchalantly. "Was it all she 'oped for as well?"

Damn his eyes! Liam heard that who-do-you-think-you're fooling tone in Harvey's voice, though he refused to rise to the bait. "Lady Seymour was most impressed by the firework display."

"Oh, aye," said the minion, obviously not the least put off by his employer's coolness. "It's a h'impressive sight right and tight. Don't wonder at anybody finding it remarkable. 'Specially not a honest, well-brought-up lady like 'er ladyship, what's spent her formative years in the country, with a respectable parson bringing 'er up proper-like, and 'im not filling 'er 'ead full of notions about gallivanting around London every year seeking worldly pleasures."

The valet paused to catch his breath and to allow for possible replies to his commentary. When no remarks were forthcoming, he continued. "If them rockets could talk, I reckon they'd be as h'impressed with Lady Seymour as she was with them. Probably give it as their opinion that she would make a gentleman what meant to spend most of his time in the country a suitable 'elpmeet." He allowed a moment for that observation to sink in. "Don't you agree, Major?"

Feeling like a rock specimen being held beneath a magnifying glass, Liam looked away from those much-too-observant gray eyes. "That will be all, thank you. I shall rise at five of the clock tomorrow."

"Yes, Major."

Felix Harvey bowed himself out of the room, but not before taking one last measuring look of his employer.

When the door finally clicked shut behind the valet, Liam just barely resisted the temptation to throw one of his patent evening shoes at the thick panel. *Suitable helpmeet* indeed! Damnation! Why did the servants always think they knew what was happening—or what a person was thinking on a particular subject—even before the person whose business it was got around to seriously considering the matter?

Wrenching his cravat from around his neck and tossing it onto the satinwood dressing table, he began to pace the room, hoping to bring some order to his jumbled mind. So much was going on inside his head—and other parts of his anatomy as well—just thinking about her. About Emaline.

Of course, he had wanted desperately to stroll down the Dark Walk with her, where he could take her in his arms and kiss her. No mere mortal man could have looked at her tonight and not wanted to do so. She had seemed at one with all that is good and beautiful in the night. The dark blue of her dress had been like the distant sky, shimmering now and then with starlight, yet cool and mysterious, promising a glimpse of the heavens. As for her coppery curls, they were touched by moonglow. And her lips . . .

He stopped his pacing. Merciful heaven! Had he really quoted poetry?

Groaning, he threw himself onto the four-poster bed, where he lay for several minutes, a pillow bunched beneath his head and his still-clad person stretched out upon the covers. It had been moon madness with him; there was no other explanation for his behavior. And yet she had been unbelievably beautiful. A pulse began to throb at the recollection of just how beautiful.

But a helpmeet? No. Out of the question. For one thing, the timing was all wrong.

Every since Toulouse—that battle waged in hell—where hunter and prey had become one and the same, and gut-wrenching vulnerability had been the lesson of the day, Liam had striven to maintain assiduous control of his life and his emotions. During the long months of his recuperation, he had drawn up a mental schedule for his days and his years, giving most attention to the creation of the Benevolent Institution and seeing that his sister was well established in the world.

What little thought he had given to his own future had included some nebulous young female of acceptable birth, whose only necessary qualifications included a biddable nature, a willingness to bear him children, and good teeth. It had suited his purpose to relegate that vague personage to a time period whose strongest appeal lay in its remoteness.

He was not ready to go looking for that suitable female. Not yet. And Felix Harvey's sentiments notwithstanding, Liam certainly had not been looking for a bride when he walked into his cousin Ambrose's dining room that afternoon almost two weeks ago and encountered Emaline. Well past the first blush of youth, and far from biddable, she had even had the effrontery to order him out of the room!

At the memory, Liam felt a smile tug the corners of his mouth. Emaline Harrison was definitely not biddable. And he could just imagine the verbal dressing down she would give any man who asked to check out her teeth!

And yet, though she was not the young lady *he* required, there was something quite special about her. Other than her beauty, and her intelligence, and her kindness, Emaline was imbued with a willingness to take life as it came and find the good in it—a quality Liam found most pleasing. In addition, she was full of energy and fun. Just being with her had brought joy back into his life.

Felix was right about one thing. She would make some man a fine helpmeet. Not to mention a warm and loving wife. Gentle and passionate, and . . .

Unbidden, the memory came to Liam of the way Emaline had swayed toward him when he held her finger to his lips. Her willingness had excited him. It had been all he could do to stop himself from grabbing her and crushing her against his chest and tasting his fill of her soft, luscious lips.

Yes, she would be passionate. Whoever she married, her husband would be the luckiest of men.

As Liam imagined Emaline melting into some man's arms, lavishing her sweetness upon some undeserving lout, he sat up, his hands bunched into fists. Unaccountably angry, he was overcome with a desire to inflict bodily harm upon the man who would be the recipient of Emaline's passion.

Unable to sit still, Liam got up off the bed and began pacing the length of the room in hopes of calming his runaway senses. At one of his turns, he remembered something that had occurred to him earlier in the evening, when he had first seen Emaline wearing the paste necklace.

Crossing the dark green carpet to the small mahogany writing desk in the corner nearest the window, he rummaged through the cubbyholes until he found paper and an inkstand with a drop or two of dark liquid remaining in its leather-covered bottle. Without taking time to sharpen the quill, he dipped the dull point into the ink, then wrote himself a reminder to have the real rubies sent to Rundall and Bridges to be cleaned, in case Emaline should choose to wear them at Cordia's ball.

With the quill still in his hand, he recalled how beautiful Emaline had looked tonight, and the alluring way in which that one coppery curl had lain against the clear white of her shoulders. The image fresh in his mind, he bent suddenly and scratched through the note. "Rubies?" he said. "Bah. Not for Emaline. Even the real thing would not do her justice. Not with her exquisite coloring."

Just before the ink dried on the quill, he wrote again, this time reminding himself to visit the jewelers as soon as he returned to town. At the bottom of the page he added: Find out if Emaline prefers emeralds or sapphires.

Chapter 13

No one in the Grosvenor Square town house got much sleep that night. Emaline had wanted to send Turner around to Cavendish Square in a hackney, but upon having it pointed out to her by the butler's tearful wife that the women would then be alone in the house, she changed her orders, telling him to go at first light.

While Turner nailed shut the French windows—Brofton's point of entry—Emaline went upstairs to compose a note to Liam explaining what had happened, and imploring him to come to them immediately. Only after the note was completed did she return to Mrs. Pruett's room to inform Cordia and the chaperone of what had happened belowstairs, leaving out nothing but the part of the story involving Turner's brother, Samuel.

"Ring for Hannah," Mrs. Pruett ordered Emaline, the instant the story was related to her. Rising unassisted from her bed, her injured leg all but forgotten, the lady hobbled around the disordered room gathering up such unmentionables as she could find and tossing them into a jumble upon the bed.

Noticing that Cordia still occupied the chair in which she had sat for the last half hour, the chaperone adjured her charge not to remain there like a bump on a log. "Time is

THE RUBY NECKLACE

wasting," she said, near-panic making her voice rise half an octave. "Hurry to your room and ring for your maid. We have not a moment to lose if we are to be packed and ready when Lord Seymour arrives. I am persuaded he will insist that you and I remove to Cavendish Square immediately."

Cordia rose from the chair, but instead of hurrying out as her chaperone had insisted, she looked at Emaline. "I—"

Emaline shook her head. She looked into the young girl's eyes; they said she was frightened and wanted to go. Though she put a brave face on it—a face that said she would stay if her friend should choose to countermand Mrs. Pruett's order.

"Perhaps it is for the best," Emaline said, giving Cordia's shoulder a reassuring squeeze. "Hannah and the Turners might wish to go as well, if you think your brother would not mind. They could remain there at least until such time as the authorities have apprehended Vernon Brofton."

The fact that she did not include her own name in the cavalcade proceeding to Cavendish Square went unnoticed by her two guests. But how could she do so? She had no claim whatever upon Liam Whitcomb. He owed her nothing, and though she could have compiled a list of things she would like to be to him, an uninvited guest was not among that number.

Remembering Lady Phoebe's none-too-subtle reference to her *hanging on Liam's sleeve,* Emaline cringed, resolving to do whatever it took to keep that from happening.

Probably the best plan for her would be to return to the place where she belonged, to Bartholsby. As before, the lack of funds for such a trip loomed before her, but if no other solution offered itself, she would ask Liam to send her home in his coach. He would attempt to encourage her to stay, of course; good breeding alone would dictate that he make an effort to convince her of her welcome in his home. But she wanted none of his proper manners.

She wanted his love. And she wanted all of it! She could admit that now . . . now that their time together was drawing to an end. She loved him, and she wanted him to love her in return. Not for just a moment, but for always. Nothing less would do.

All her fine talk of wishing to experience passion for its sake alone was just that—talk. Emaline still wanted the passion, and she knew Liam could give her what she wanted, but she had come to realize that the reason he, and he alone, roused such emotions in her was because she loved him. Loved him with all her soul, all her spirit. Never mind that he was a *premier parti* and she a country nobody. She had given him her heart, and it could never be recalled.

How it had happened, or when it had happened, mattered little. Somewhere in their meetings she had come to love him, and knowing that his feelings for her were no more than those of one friend for another, she did not believe she could endure being under the same roof with him.

Her only alternative was to return to Bartholsby. With that thought in mind, she left Cordia and Mrs. Pruett to their packing and returned to her own room to gather her belongings. Unfortunately, the task required less time than she would have thought possible, and even less concentration, leaving her mind free to dwell on Liam and the love she bore him.

What little time remained of the night, Emaline spent sitting in a slipper chair pulled up to the dressing-room windows. With her night rail covered by an old shawl of her mother's, and her feet tucked beneath her, she leaned her head against the cool panes of glass and gazed up at the heavens. At one point she made a wish upon a particularly bright star, but being a woman of seven and twenty, and supposedly much too mature for such foolishness, she did not delude herself that her wish might come true.

By the time morning light turned the sky from darkest blue to gray, then from gray to pink, Emaline had determined upon a course of action. Considering her firm belief in doing the right thing, while being willing to accept heavenly intervention, she decided not to act precipitously. First she would listen to any suggestions Liam made regarding the properest thing to do about Vernon Brofton. Then, if there were no action she needed to take to bring the man to justice, she would ask Liam to send her home to Wiltshire.

She would watch him carefully while she made the request. If he bowed politely and agreed to send the carriage around, she would know exactly where she stood. But— and this caveat was issued with both a prayer and crossed fingers—if he made a counter-suggestion, one that even *hinted* at his wanting more time to see if they had a future together, she would stay.

Comfortable with this plan, she left her chair by the window and hurriedly donned one of her new dresses, wanting to look her best when Liam arrived. Even allowing for the fact that she had not slept at all, one glance in her looking glass told her that the pale pistache of the crisp challis frock, with its collar of blond lace, was a wise choice. The shimmering green cheered her, making her feel as fresh and hopeful as springtime.

Unfortunately, that hopeful outlook was sorely tested when Turner returned from his errand not in Liam's coach, but in the hackney carriage hired to take him to Cavendish Square.

"His lordship is not at home," the butler informed her, his own disappointment as deeply felt as hers. "He left about an hour before I arrived. Something to do with a ground-breaking ceremony of some kind in a little village south of Merton. Went down in the berline, so his valet said, on account of it giving a more formal appearance."

Emaline sank onto the beige settee where she had been waiting for the last half hour. Suddenly she was very tired, the lack of sleep catching up with her and making her feel dull-witted and lethargic. "Last evening Lord Seymour said something about leaving town for a few days, but I never dreamed he would depart before daybreak."

Closing her eyes, she put her fingertips to her temples, which had begun to throb. *If only I had sent Turner around last night instead of giving in to his wife's pleading.*

But what good were *if onlys*? They held one back. They got in the way, acting as stumbling blocks to the formulation of new plans. Not that Emaline could think of anything new! Not now; not with her head pounding as though miniature carpenters were inside it, building barricades against the escape of practical thoughts.

"The valet," Turner continued, "though not a true gentleman's gentleman by any means, was most helpful."

"Harvey?" Emaline asked, opening her eyes at the recollection of the feisty little valet. "Did he not go with Lord Seymour?"

"No, my lady. Mr. Harvey was to follow at a more leisurely pace with the curricle, so when I told him it was quite important that Lord Seymour get your message as soon as possible, he agreed to deliver it directly the ceremonies were over."

The throbbing in Emaline's temples abated, and she sat up, her mind working again. "Good thinking, Turner. Perhaps it will serve. How far is it to this little village? Do you know?"

"That I cannot say, my lady, but the trip to Merton wants something under two hours. Depending upon the traffic and the weather and the general condition of the roads, of course."

While Emaline digested this information, trying to estimate the number of hours needed to travel there and back, plus the time necessary to complete the ceremony, the noise upon the stairs signaled the descent of Mrs. Pruett, assisted by Cordia and her maid.

"Where is Lord Seymour?" the chaperone demanded after scanning the entire room for proof of his presence. "Why has he not come? Did you not send for him?"

Not waiting for a reply, the agitated lady continued, her voice growing more strident with each word. "How very remiss of you, to be sure, for how are we to go on with no gentleman to tell us what we must do?"

"Be quiet!" Emaline said, every bit as wishful of seeing that knight in shining armor as was the chaperone, but tired beyond reason of such histrionics. "I cannot think with you carrying on like the veriest goose."

After a gasp, the frightened lady resorted to her handkerchief, muttering between sniffs that they should all count themselves fortunate if they were not found murdered at the dinner table.

"Well, you shall not be," Emaline said, "at least not at *this* dinner table. For I was just telling Turner to find a hackney to convey you and Cordia to Cavendish Square."

Turning to the butler, she said, "Let us know the minute the carriage is here."

"Yes, my lady."

Within seconds they could hear Turner out on the street, whistling for the jarvey.

"There will be room for only the three of you in the

hackney," Emaline said, "so you will need to leave your baggage here for the time being. When Lord Seymour returns, he will see to the details."

Taking Cordia's hand in hers, she gave it a squeeze. "Do not worry; all will be well."

Cordia blinked in surprise, as if only just realizing that her friend was not dressed for a carriage ride. "But what of you? Are you not coming with us?"

Emaline shook her head. "Not yet, in any event. There is something important I must discover first."

"The hackney is here, my lady."

"Thank you, Turner. If you will be so kind, please give Mrs. Pruett your arm down the front steps."

While the butler and the maid helped the chaperone out to the carriage, Cordia turned and threw her arms around Emaline's neck, hugging her tightly. "Please come," she begged.

"I cannot." Disentangling herself from the embrace, she said, "But thank you for asking."

"Has your reluctance anything to do with my brother?"

Emaline was tempted to deny it, but reconsidered. "It has everything to do with him."

"I feared that was so. Please believe me when I tell you that he would want you to come with us. He is very much in . . . concerned about you."

Emaline's spirits soared at what the chit had almost said. *She believes her brother loves me.* For a moment that was enough to give her hope. But only for a moment.

Placing her arm around Cordia's shoulder, she turned the young lady and ushered her to the door. "This is not something you and I should discuss."

"But—"

"If it is to be, it will be. But whatever the truth of the situation, I must hear it from your brother's lips."

The hackney had been gone less than an hour when the knocker sounded at the front entrance. Emaline jumped at the sound, but after reasoning that Brofton was hardly likely to seek entrance at the front door, and certainly would not do so in broad daylight, she bid the anxious butler see who it was.

Returning minutes later, his dignity very much offended, he informed her, "The *person* claims to have something of importance to tell you."

"Has this person a name?"

"One assumes so, my lady. However, she insists you will know her simply as Agnes."

Though quite surprised that Agnes should choose to call upon her, Emaline assured the butler that she would see the visitor. "Show her in here, please."

Turner did as he was bid, but he did not deign to announce the caller, merely opening the drawing room door, then stepping aside to allow her entry.

Emaline crossed the room, her hand extended in greeting. "What a surprise, to be sure. Do come in. May I offer you some refreshment?"

The disarmingly tall feathers upon the wide-poked purple bonnet swayed back and forth as the visitor shook her head. "This ain't a social call, your ladyship. Not that I don't thank you ever so for treatin' it like it was. Still and all, I've come because I discovered something I believe you should know."

Emaline motioned her to the settee, then pulled up one of the gold rococo chairs for herself. "What is it?" she asked.

After taking a moment to unbutton her purple plush

pelisse, the visitor got right to the point. "Last night, after me and Johnny Barham left Vauxhall, we decided to stop for a pint at The Two Rams, it being just a hop and a skip from my place, and—." She stopped, her face turning a red that rivaled her orange hair. "What I mean to say is, we was sitting at a table, minding our own business, just wetting our whistles, when who should come stomping in but that nasty, weasel-faced yahoo what used to valet for Lord Seymour. May his lordship rest in peace," she added quietly.

Emaline laced her fingers together to keep them from trembling. Something told her she did not want to hear the whole story. "Brofton," she said.

"Yes. That's his name. Not but what *Gallows Bird* wouldn't suit him better, seeing as that's where he's headed, or I miss my guess."

"You are quite astute."

"Well, as to that," she replied, blushing furiously, "I do try to keep my eyes and ears open. That's how I come to overhear old weasel-face telling this other fellow how he was looking for someone to help him with a job of work. A job involving getting back something he claims belonged to him in the first place."

Emaline's mouth went very dry. "A necklace?"

"Well, now," Agnes said, her eyes wide with surprise, "seems like you're a real 'stute yourself."

"Did the other man agree to help him?"

Agnes shook her head, imperiling the feathers once again. "The other chap said he didn't risk his neck with blokes he hadn't known from the cradle. Much less them as said they didn't care who they had to kill, long as the job got done."

Licking suddenly sand-dry lips, Emaline asked if the

man had mentioned the name of that person whose life was expendable.

"Your ladyship being so 'stute and all," she said very softly, "I collect you'll know the name without me having to say it."

"Mine?" Emaline asked, the word a whisper.

"Yes. The scoundrel said, 'Lady Seymour.'"

"The shop is just around the next corner," Agnes yelled to the hackney driver, "but the street's too narrow for a carriage. Pull up anyplace. We'll walk the rest of the way."

After climbing down from the carriage, its floor strewn with foul-smelling straw, she took the pound note Emaline was about to bestow upon the jarvey and tore it in two, giving the man one half and tucking the other half inside her lilac kid glove. "You'll get the rest of this if you're waiting here when we get back. Otherwise . . ." She shrugged her shoulders to show her indifference.

"I said I'd wait," the man grumbled. "A fine thing when an honest man's word ain't good enough for the likes of—"

"Let's go," Agnes said, grabbing Emaline by the arm and more or less propelling her down the narrow street. "And you remember what I told your ladyship. Don't go looking nobody in the eye, and don't speak unless I tell you to."

"I will do as you say. And thank you again for your help. I should never have known how to do this."

"Save your thanks until we see if old Gaspar is willing to deal. He doesn't ask questions about the origin of a person's merchandise, but if he takes you in dislike, he won't do business."

Emaline had no idea where they were, except that it was somewhere in the East End, and that the streets were so crowded with humanity she was constantly jostled and bumped into by peddlers calling out their wares—shouting everything from matches to rat poison—while costermongers extolled the beauty of their fruits and vegetables, and children too numerous to count and far too dirty to touch begged for pennies.

Just past a dark, mean-looking alleyway, Agnes opened a shop door and pushed Emaline inside. "Gaspar," she called into the eerie dimness, once the door was shut and a goodly portion of the daylight and the street noise was obliterated, "are you here? I've brought a customer for you."

Liam squirmed in his seat while the local squire described him with such extravagant praise that he wondered why the entire audience did not rise *en masse* and rebel at the excess.

"A fine Surrey gentleman," the squire proclaimed loudly, "and one who served his country well. A soldier himself. Nay! a hero. Wounded in the battle of . . ."

Closing his ears to the man's never-ending introduction, Liam looked about him at the cleared acreage and the four gold-painted stakes protruding from the ground, representing the four corners of the soon-to-be-constructed Benevolent Institution. In the distance, tall oaks stood watch over coppiced birch and hazel—their remaining trunks forming little woodland stools—while turtle doves and cuckoos flew about from limb to limb.

With his thoughts occupied by the beauty of the countryside, and how much he would like to show it all to Emaline, he experienced a sudden start when he saw Felix Harvey at the back of the crowd. Something was wrong. Without any rhyme or reason, he knew it was so. Unfortunately, when he would have signaled to his valet to come forward, the squire finally ended his interminable introduction and sat down. Amid the welcoming applause and the shouts of, "Hear! Hear!" Liam rose, approached the speaker's podium, and delivered his short speech.

It was not to be expected that the audience of villagers and local veterans would allow their hero to speak and run. Everyone wanted to shake his hand and tell him how pleased they were to have such a fine new building going up in their neighborhood, so it was close to an hour before Liam managed to discover why Felix had come.

"From 'er ladyship," he said, passing Emaline's letter to Liam. "H'important, so 'er butler said."

Ripping open the seal, Liam scanned the hurriedly written note, swore under his breath, then read every word a second time. Certain now of his grasp of the situation, he felt a cold hand reach inside his chest and squeeze the life out of his heart. "I must return to town immediately," he said, surprised that his words could sound so calm when his very life's blood seemed frozen in his veins. "Lady Seymour is in danger."

"I suspected something was amiss, Major, so I took the liberty of 'aving fresh 'orses 'itched to the curricle." He pointed some hundred yards beyond the crowd, where a youth held a restive pair in check.

"Good man."

As they quick-stepped their way toward the carriage, Liam said, "Make my apologies to the gentlemen of the committee, and explain to them why I could not stay for tea and cakes—an illness in the family should suffice as reason for my leaving so abruptly—then meet me back in town as soon as possible. You will find the berline at the local blacksmith's."

"Yes, Major."

After flipping a gold coin to the youth holding the

horses, Liam sprang up into the curricle, bid the lad step aside, then gave the horses the signal to be on their way. Within minutes, they were galloping toward the road to London.

Emaline counted the pound notes for the third time, still unsure if the entire transaction had taken place, or if it was a dream from which she would awaken at any moment. Had she really accompanied a woman of questionable reputation to a moneylender? And not just any moneylender, but one who, according to Agnes, struck fear in the hearts of every man, woman, and child in the East End.

What on earth would her papa say if he knew the lengths to which she had gone to acquire enough money to purchase her passage home to Bartholsby? She had accepted thirty pounds in exchange for a necklace that might not even belong to her, yet somehow the question of ownership bothered her less than the amount of the money. For a parson's daughter, thirty had an unpleasant connotation, making her feel as though she were betraying someone.

"Only myself," she said. She wanted desperately to wait for Liam's return, to see if he did indeed love her, but fear held her in its grip. What if Brofton arrived first?

"You tell old weasel-face," Agnes had instructed her just before they parted company, "that you gave the necklace to Gaspar. Tell him if he wants it, to go get it." The woman rolled her eyes heavenward. "Any that's got brains in their nous box will steer clear of Gaspar, but if it's trouble Brofton wants, it's trouble he shall have."

After leaving the moneylender's, Agnes had taken Emaline to a booking office to procure a ticket to Wiltshire. Once her name, boarding point, destination, and amount of fare paid were entered on the waybill, Emaline thanked the woman for her help and her kindness, then the two went their separate ways. Agnes took a hackney back to her flat to sleep away whatever remained of the daylight hours, while Emaline traveled back to Seymour House to get her belongings.

Reluctantly, Emaline alighted from the hackney, paid her fare, then slowly climbed the front steps. She wished she did not have to reenter the town house, but unlike Cordia and Mrs. Pruett, she could not leave her clothes until later. Returning to Bartholsby would be difficult enough for her; to do so with only the clothes on her back would be to incite the kind of gossip that would ruin her for good.

"Besides," she muttered, "the servants are still here."

She had no more than voiced the statement when she began to suspect otherwise, for no one answered her knock. After several minutes, she returned to the pavement and descended the half-dozen steps that went below street level to the service entrance. The kitchen door was shut but not locked. Opening it slowly, she crossed the scrubbed stone floor, stopping beside the sturdy deal table where she had sat drinking coffee late last night.

This time, the table showed no signs of hurried departure. In fact, the entire kitchen was neat to a fault. The dishes were all washed and stacked in the dresser cupboard, the pans were scoured and hanging from the ceiling, and even the dishpan had been emptied and turned over to drain dry. The stove, when she touched it, was cold.

Taking one quick, nervous peek into the larder, and finding it empty of humankind, Emaline decided the servants had not waited for her return. They were gone. Wishing she could say the same for herself, she returned to the table, leaning her hands against it to steady her shaking knees.

This was idiocy, she decided. It was scarce three in the

afternoon. Any fool knew that evildoers waited for the cover of darkness to go skulking about other people's houses. By that time, she would be at The Swan, boarding the mail coach for Wiltshire.

Calling herself a ninnyhammer, Emaline bolted the service entrance. Then, crossing to the wooden door that opened onto the corridor, she climbed the six stone steps and let herself into the main portion of the house.

As she hurried up the stairs to her bedchamber, she tried not to look over her shoulder more than once every fifteen seconds. Taking into consideration the depth of her fear and the fact that there were no servants to help her take her things down to the street, Emaline decided she would make do with only one valise. The rest of her luggage could be sent to her at a later time.

Not wishing to delay her exit by so much as the five seconds needed to glance into her looking glass to see if her bonnet was on straight, she opened the door and stepped out onto the landing. Her foot had only just touched the top step when she heard the window pane shatter in the library.

Chapter 14

Paralyzed with fear, Emaline stood at the top of the stairs, listening to the splintering of the French windows as they were kicked in. Within seconds, when she heard the sound of heavy shoes crunching over the broken glass, her heart began to beat so loudly she pressed her hand to her chest in an effort to still the noise.

What should she do? Like most young ladies, during her young years she had been adjured not to run, and as a consequence, she lacked both the skill and the nerve to make a dash for the front entrance. And even if she were faster than whoever waited belowstairs, the door was bolted. By the time she got it open, the intruder would be upon her.

But she could not just stand here like a frightened hare, waiting to become the next meal for whatever bigger, stronger animal chose to pounce upon her. She would not! Emaline Harrison was made of sterner stuff! If someone wanted her for dinner, they would jolly well have to find her first.

Tiptoeing back to her bedroom, she shoved her valise beneath the bed, then looked about her for a place to hide. Remembering that Brofton had searched this chamber from top to bottom the evening before, and afraid he might do so again, she decided her best chance for concealment was to go higher.

Aware that she would be hampered by her pelisse and bonnet, she paused long enough to remove the confining garments and shove them and her reticule beneath the bed. As well, she removed her half-boots before creeping across the landing to the next flight of stairs. Stealthy as a mouse, she stole past Mrs. Pruett's bedroom, then continued to the final landing, which gave access to four small attic rooms, one of which was used by the maid, Hannah. Just beyond those sleeping quarters, tucked beneath the gabled roof, was the storage room.

Having rummaged through that particular space dozens of times while rearranging the drawing-room furniture, Emaline was familiar with the squeak in the first of the three scarred plank steps. Congratulating herself on recollecting the treacherous spot, she lifted her skirt and took a giant stride to the second step.

It needed only a single turn of the large iron key that was always left in the lock, and Emaline was inside the dusty, cobwebbed storage room. She resisted the urge to open the dormer window to let in air and light, for logic told her that the semidarkness was her ally. At the same time, however, the discarded furniture, shrouded in Holland covers, whispered illogically that she had entered the domain of ghosts.

Foolish beyond permission!

Refusing to lose command of her emotions, Emaline took a steadying breath, then looked around her, allowing her more rational self a moment to recognize and name the pieces of shrouded furniture. One of the two ghosts to the right was the heavy leather wing chair Liam had sat in the first day he came to take her for a drive, the day he had called the drawing room a mausoleum. To the left was that game table with the broken leg.

There was nothing to be frightened of here. All she need worry about was the man whose footsteps were being cushioned by the carpeting on the first landing.

With her ear pressed against the door, she heard numerous bumps and thuds, as though the man were turning over pieces of furniture in hers and Cordia's bedchambers. Minutes later she heard similar noises on the next level. Within a frighteningly short span of time, footsteps echoed on the uncarpeted upper floor as he made a quick search of the servants' sleeping quarters.

Realizing it was just a matter of time before he stormed the storage room, Emaline tiptoed over to the wing chair and lifted back the Holland cover, praying the dust would not cause her to sneeze. After saying a brief prayer that she was doing the right thing, she curled up in the chair with her feet tucked under her. After hurriedly wedging the hem of her skirt beneath her knees and legs so it would not escape and betray her whereabouts, she eased the white sheeting back over her head and body, and the arms and body of the chair.

The plank squeaked, and Emaline pressed her fist against her mouth to stay the scream that longed to escape.

Into the stillness that followed the squeak, Vernon Brofton called out, "All ye, all ye urchins free." The menacing sing-song of the childhood phrase sent shivers down Emaline's spine. "Come out, come out, wherever you are."

As the door was flung open, the sudden draft caused the thick cover to move slightly, making Emaline fear instant detection. Such was not the case, however, for the man stomped about the room, pushing furniture aside and making a thoroughly noisy job of checking out any item large enough to offer a hiding place.

"I saw you get out of the hackney," Brofton said, only inches away from the wing chair. "I'd been waiting for you to return."

Suddenly, Emaline felt the wing chair being tipped backward. Her stomach pitched sickeningly as he held the chair suspended above the floor for several seconds, like a cat playing with a mouse, before he set it upright again.

"You like games?" he asked, his face so close to hers she could feel his hot breath through the sheeting. "I've got one we can play. Ready to give it a go?"

Emaline's heart jumped into her throat, and she could not have answered him if her life depended on it.

"What I've got in mind," he said, "is for you to—"

"I like games," said an angry voice from the doorway. "Perhaps you should challenge me instead."

"You!"

"Step away from that chair," Liam ordered, "or I will blow your head off."

Brofton laughed, the diabolical sound reverberating in the small enclosure. "There's heads and then there's heads," he said.

Before Emaline realized what was happening, the valet had caught her up, sheet and all, and yanked her against him. Something small and round was pressed against her forehead, and even without seeing it, she knew it was the bore of a pistol.

"Got any more orders to give?" Brofton asked. He laughed again. "You see, if we play, we play by my rules." The laugh turned into a growl. "Now drop the barker."

Emaline heard something land with a thud on the plank steps and knew it was Liam's weapon.

"Let her go," Liam said quietly. "Lady Seymour does not have the ruby necklace."

A stream of curses greeted this announcement, then Brofton said, "You think me an idgit? I know she's got it. I saw it in this house not two days ago."

"You were mistaken," Liam said, "the rubies are—"

"I have them!" Emaline yelled, suddenly gripped with a fear more intense than any she had felt before. She could not let Liam inform this crazed monster that *he* was in possession of the real ruby necklace. Brofton was willing to kill for the jewels, and she would rather die herself than let Liam be killed.

The valet had held her captive with his arm wrapped around her arms and chest, the Holland cover assisting him in confining her. But now he slid his arm up to her neck, tightening his hold until she thought she would faint from lack of air. "Give 'em here," he muttered into her ear, "or I'll snap your scrawny neck like a pigeon bone, then I'll shoot his high-and-mighty lordship right between the eyes."

"I told you," Liam began, "that I—"

"I took them to a moneylender!"

Brofton gave her neck a vicious squeeze. "Don't you lie to me."

"I am telling the truth. The receipt is in my reticule, along with the money he gave me."

"Give it here!"

"It is under my bed. I hid it when I heard you coming."

"You'd best not be telling me lies," he warned, giving her neck a cruel yank.

She heard Liam curse. "Leave her be, or I'll—"

"You'll what?" Brofton said, taking a step to the right and pulling Emaline with him. "Jump me? Mill me down?

Not unless you want to see her ladyship's claret stain this nice Holland cover."

Still holding Emaline by the neck, he stepped sideways until he encountered a piece of furniture and could go no farther. "You!" he shouted to Liam. "Get over there by that window. And no tricks, mind. I'd as soon shoot you as not."

The sound of Liam's boots crossing the wooden floor told Emaline he had followed the valet's order.

"Now," Brofton said, dragging Emaline to the space Liam had just vacated, "you and me'll go get that receipt."

Before she knew what he was about, he shoved her down the three plank steps, slammed the door, and turned the iron key, locking Liam inside. Emaline lay upon the hard floor, her heart pounding and her eyes wet with tears of relief. *Liam was unharmed.* Whatever happened now, she could endure it, knowing the man she loved was safe.

Brofton yanked away the Holland cover, then jerked her to her feet. In little more than a minute, they were back in her bedchamber, with her down on all fours retrieving the reticule from beneath the bed.

"This better not be some tarradiddle," he warned her.

With hands so shaky she doubted her ability to make them work, Emaline freed the strings of the reticule and dumped its contents onto the carpet in front of her. The moneylender's receipt was the last to fall free, landing atop the thirty pound notes, a linen handkerchief, and several copper coins.

Pushing her aside, Brofton snatched up the paper and read the description of the property used as collateral for the loan. "At last," he said, his fleshy lips pulled into a travesty of a smile, "I will finally get what is mine."

He bent to retrieve the money, then stuffed it and the

paper into his coat pocket. Without another glance in Emaline's direction, the valet turned and left the room.

Liam heard the blackguard push Emaline down the steps then turn the key in the door, and though he longed to throttle the cur with his own hands, he could do nothing without risking further injury to Emaline. Not now, in any case.

Rage boiled inside him as he pictured all the terrible things the man might do to her. Things Liam was momentarily powerless to stop. He had erred in his frontal attack. Vernon Brofton was no soldier trained in the arts of war; he was a hoodlum from the London streets. A hoodlum who enjoyed his brutal little games, making no distinction between warrior and civilian, using the defenseless to disarm the strong.

Cursing himself for his error in judgment, Liam planned his next encounter. First he must get out of the storage room, then he must find Emaline without revealing his presence to Brofton. And when he found them, he would do whatever it took to free her. This time he would forget the lessons taught him as an officer and a gentleman; this time he would beat the hoodlum at his own game.

With his ear to the door, he listened until Brofton and Emaline were beyond the attic rooms and on the stairs headed toward the lower floors, then he hurried to the dormer window and threw up the sash.

Being slender, he was able to crawl through the opening with very little trouble. However, crossing the shingled roof, even for the few feet necessary to reach the first of the attic bedrooms, was something he hoped never to do again—especially when the roof was five stories above the pavement.

Pushing open the window to the sparsely furnished

chamber, he entered the room head first, rolling when he hit the floor and coming to his feet within seconds. Although his breathing was a bit uneven, his soldier's training had taken over and he was ready to confront the enemy.

As it transpired, the confrontation took place sooner than he had envisioned. Descending the stairs quietly, his back to the wall, Liam spied Brofton coming from what he assumed was the master bedchamber. The man was overconfident—always a mistake, even with an enemy who appeared to be no longer a threat—for he looked to neither right nor left but hurried down the stairs toward the vestibule.

Seizing the opportunity, Liam sped across the landing toward the valet. Before Brofton had time to react to the noise behind him, Liam grabbed the bannister, holding it firmly while he leapt into the air. Both booted feet made contact, hitting the valet a telling blow to the shoulder and back and making him pitch forward down the steps.

Still holding to the bannister, Liam pulled himself to his feet. At the bottom of the stairs, Brofton lay sprawled across the vestibule floor, unmoving, and quiet as death. Giving the valet only a momentary glance, Liam dashed across the landing to push open the door to the bedchamber. Emaline sat on the floor, her face whiter than the sheeting that had covered her when he saw her last. "Emaline!"

"Liam!"

Needing no further encouragement, he closed the space between them, pulling her to her feet and into his arms, holding her as though he meant never to let her go. As she returned his frantic embrace, Liam closed his eyes while a near-shattering wave of relief washed over him.

After a time, he loosened his hold on her, wanting to see her, to assure himself that she was unharmed. Though he looked her over from head to toe, his mind seemed incapable of coherent thought. Unable to recall any of the questions he had wanted to ask when he feared for her life, when he was afraid he might never see her again, Liam dismissed them all. There would be time for questions later. For the moment, at least, he was content to take Emaline's dust-smeared face between his hands, satisfying his immediate need by letting his gaze caress her mouth, her cheeks, her eyes.

"My love," he murmured, his voice husky with mingled fear and relief. "My sweet love."

Chapter 15

Unsure if she had actually heard the words, or if she had only imagined them, Emaline asked rather breathlessly, "Am I, Liam? Am I your love?"

Whatever his answer might have been, she was not to know it that day, for when he would have spoken, they both heard the unmistakable scrape of a metal bolt being yanked free. An instant later a loud crash told them the front door had been thrown wide, slamming against the wall.

"Stay here!" Liam ordered. Without waiting for her reply, he dashed out to the landing and bounded down the stairs.

Ignoring his instruction, Emaline followed right behind him. Of course, she could not run anywhere near as fast as Liam. Hampered not only by her skirts but also by the fact that she was without shoes, she arrived at the front steps in time to see Liam turn the corner of the block, running at full speed. In less than a minute, however, he returned.

"Brofton got away," he said, his words clipped, his blue eyes dark with anger. "Like the vermin he is, the rat found some hole in which to hide."

Emaline could not bring herself to care that the valet had escaped. She was too happy to be alive, and far too happy to have Liam by her side, unharmed, to give a thought to what became of Vernon Brofton.

"Come," Liam said, taking her arm and leading her toward his curricle and the wide-eyed lad who stood at the horses' heads, his mouth hanging open in amazement at the spectacle he had just witnessed. "You are going to Cavendish Square."

Emaline had almost allowed him to help her into the carriage when she stopped suddenly, noticing the gawking lad and imagining how very odd she must appear after the events of the last half hour. Glancing at her hands and her frock, she found them liberally covered with soot. After a cursory examination of her hair, she discovered the once-neat coiffure felt like a veritable bird's nest as a result of hiding beneath the Holland covers. Added to that deplorable condition was the fact that she was shoeless, hatless, and without anything save the filthy dress upon her back. "I cannot drive through the streets like this!" she protested. "I must return for my valise and my hat."

Disinclined to argue, Liam swept her off her feet and set her in the carriage. After tossing a guinea to the lad, he jumped up on the box beside her.

"Wait!" Emaline protested as the curricle began to move, "I did not lock the door." Giving little heed to her words, Liam urged the horses forward, never once looking back at the town house.

It was a full two days before Emaline saw Liam again. Within minutes of their arrival in Cavendish Square, where they were greeted by the horrified cries of Cordia and the well-timed swoon of Mrs. Pruett, Liam had packed his bags and removed to Grillon's Hotel, at number 7 Albemarle Street. Before his departure, however, he had seen to the securing of the rented town house, reassuring the three female inhabitants that they would come to no harm, being guarded by two butlers, a strong young footman, a well-armed Felix Harvey, and round-the-clock Bow Street Runners.

All this security notwithstanding, Emaline was restless, unable to relax. She yearned for Liam's return. Too much had been left unsaid between them, and as each new hour passed, she was torn between her desire to believe that Liam loved her, and her fear that she had embellished their brief encounter beyond all resemblance to the truth.

Both days Emaline had sat in the first-floor drawing room, the door left ajar so she would not miss the arrival of any visitor. On the first day, no one had even approached the front door, but on the second she heard the knocker echo through the corridor. At the sound, Emaline held her breath. Her heart very nearly escaped her chest while she waited to hear the caller speak.

Sadly, the voice was not Liam's.

Though disappointment made her long to scream, or throw something, or both—anything to relieve the tension that was building inside her—she was obliged to school her face to a welcoming smile when Turner announced the visitor.

"Captain Beauchamp," she said, extending her hand in greeting, "how do you do?"

"Lady Seymour—Emaline," he said, saluting her knuckles with a brief kiss. "It is so nice of you to receive me."

"Not at all, sir, for I am heartily blue-deviled with my own company. If the truth be known, after being a virtual prisoner in the house, with little news of the outside world, I should be pleased to entertain Napoleon himself. You, I welcome with open arms."

Taking this statement in good part, Captain Beauchamp smiled. At her invitation, he seated himself upon one of the gold brocade chairs that gave the first-floor chamber its designation as the yellow withdrawing room.

When he crossed one elegant leg over the other, Emaline's attention was called to the fact that he looked particularly handsome, almost as if he were dressed for some special task. His dark hair was newly trimmed, his Hessians were polished to a brilliant shine, his shirt points were crisp and pristine white, and his cravat had been tied to nicety. As well, over his snug fitting, biscuit-hued pantaloons, he wore a pale blue driving coat whose color gave his gray eyes the look of a cool mountain lake.

"Champ," she said, dismissing whatever important mission he may have come upon and getting right to the subject uppermost in her mind. "Have you seen Liam?"

"Not today. But I was with him all of yesterday and most of last evening."

"Did he—" she wanted to ask if Liam had mentioned coming to see her, but at the last moment she decided the question would embarrass Champ as much as it would her. "Did you see Brofton?" she asked instead.

"He is dead, you know. No need to give him another thought."

"Yes. I had heard of his demise."

Emaline had picked up her needlework, but she returned it to the table beside her own gold chair, its calming influence rendered ineffectual by the mention of Vernon Brofton. "Liam sent us a message by one of the Runners, but he gave none of the particulars. Do you know what happened?"

"Only the barest bones. Liam and I were at the Bow Street headquarters when a rather seedy-looking fellow came in to lay an information against a certain East End moneylender."

"Gaspar?" Emaline asked, apprehension making her heart race. "I was worried about him."

"Wasted concern ma'am, I assure you. The man is a known criminal, well able to look out for himself."

"That is what Agnes said, yet I could not help but feel guilty about giving Brofton the receipt, knowing his obsession with the necklace, and that he would try to get it from the moneylender any way he could. Is Gaspar all right?"

Champ shrugged his broad shoulders. "Who can say? From all Liam and I discovered of the man, he is a cat with nine lives, so I would not worry overmuch about his health if I were you."

"You did not see him? Gaspar, I mean."

"No. When we arrived at that dingy little shop of his, we found only Brofton. The valet was lying on the floor, his pistol in one hand, the receipt for the necklace in the other, and a knife sticking out of his chest. As for the moneylender, my guess is that he is residing in some thieves' den not unlike his own establishment, just biding his time, waiting until everyone forgets about the murder so he can return to business as usua—"

"Devil take it!" Champ muttered under his breath, only just noticing that Emaline had pressed her handkerchief to her lips and was swallowing with difficulty. "Forgive me. I should not have told you the sordid details."

"It . . . it is all right. I needed to hear them. Until this moment I do not think I really believed that Brofton was dead. Now I can stop looking over my shoulder, expecting him to materialize at any moment. I thank you for telling me the whole."

"You are kind to be so understanding," he said, "but I should have kept my tongue between my teeth. I fear mine are soldier's manners."

"If stating the truth is soldier's manners, then I can find no fault with them."

"That is because you are not obliged to endure them for long periods."

He smiled his rogue's smile. "My sister despairs of my ever relearning the ways of a gentleman. Of course, it could be her shyness that makes her overly nice in her notions. Which is why," he added, "that I am pleased she has decided to have Fitzhugh. He may not talk much, but Fitz's manners are impeccable. Got good *ton* too."

Happy to give her thoughts a new direction, Emaline asked if she had understood him aright. "Has Mary formed a *tendre* for Mr. Fitzhugh?"

"More like she has given in to the inevitable."

"I beg your pardon?"

"Fitz has only been waiting for my sister's come-out to declare himself. Been running tame in our house since he was in short coats. He and Mary were playfellows, don't you know, and there was never anyone for him but her. I daresay the same is true for Mary. If I know anything of the matter, they will deal extremely with one another."

Much struck by this piece of information, Emaline asked how Lady Phoebe felt upon the subject. "For I had thought her ladyship cherished hopes of a more worldly connection for your sister."

"Angling for a title, you mean?" Champ laughed aloud. "That was never Mary's ambition. Nor my father's. And if he had known, he would have put a stop to that nonsense about seeking a title before my mother ever left for town."

Emaline tried to keep her expression from revealing her astonishment that anyone could check the imperious Lady Phoebe.

"In any case," Champ continued, "our mother will just

have to content herself with the knowledge that her daughter is to wed one of the wealthiest men in the kingdom. Fitz's father is rich as Croesus, don't you know."

Their discussion of the happy couple was interrupted by the arrival of the butler. "I took the liberty of ordering tea, my lady."

Her concern for Liam having left Emaline without appetite for two days, she turned her face away from the assortment of delicacies arranged attractively in a silver cake basket, motioning for Turner to set the basket close to Champ. "I cannot offer you sugared sponge cakes, which I understand are your favorites," she said, "but perhaps you might like to try some of Mrs. Turner's scones. They are what my father would have called 'magic for one's mouth,' owing to the speed with which they are made to disappear."

Though her guest smiled at the little joke, he declined the tea, seeming suddenly to have become ill at ease. "Actually, ma'am, with the danger from Brofton at an end, I had hoped I might discover if Miss Cor—that to say, if either of you ladies would like to go for a turn around the park. I have my curricle just outside, with a tiger up behind for the proprieties."

So. That is the purpose of Champ's handsome attire. He has taken the bull by the horns and come to call upon Cordia. And with a chaperone, no less!

Schooling her face to blandness, Emaline informed him that she had *far* too many tasks that wanted doing to go out, but she adjured the butler to inform Miss Cordia that Captain Beauchamp had arrived. "Tell her, please, Turner, that the captain especially wished to know if she would go for a drive with him."

"I shall send the maid up immediately, my lady."

His mission put to the test at last, Champ seemed to recover his usual good spirits, relaxing enough to avail himself of a plum tart. While they waited for Cordia's arrival, he beguiled the time by regaling Emaline with an amusing story about a much younger Mr. Fitzhugh and a certain mean-spirited goose that was used to belong to their cook.

He had arrived at a particularly funny segment of the story—one involving a dash across a meadow, with his future brother-in-law running for his life, pursued by the hissing goose—when the door swung open and Lord Seymour stepped into the drawing room.

Emaline's heart did a somersault. And although she was at that moment brushing away the tears of laughter that stained her cheeks, Champ's story was forgotten on the instant. Seeing Liam standing in the doorway, his slender person so elegant and his blond hair like sunshine come to earth, she would have consigned Captain Beauchamp to the antipodes without a qualm. Anything to be alone with the man she loved.

"Liam, old son," Champ said, "come join us. I was just telling Emaline about the time a goose chased Fitz across one of our meadows."

A sardonic smile played upon Liam's face. "At least Fitzhugh had the good sense to know when he was not wanted. You, on the other hand, seem lacking in such instincts for preservation."

"Ecod, man! I thought we got that all settled yesterday."

"So did I." Liam brushed an infinitesimal speck from the sleeve of his bottle-green coat. "I hope," he said affably, "that I shall not have to run you through with my sword."

Champ laughed, not the least bit intimidated by his friend's threat. "No need for such drastic measures, old son. I can take a hint. You wish me otherwhere, and I will gladly go." He cleared his throat. "Just as soon as Miss Cordia arrives."

Liam looked from his friend to Emaline. "What has my sister to say of the matter?"

Emaline chose to answer the question, not altogether comfortable with this masculine exchange. "Champ has come to take Cordia for a drive in the park."

Still not convinced, Liam said, "Why would he wish to take my little sister anypl—"

"Because," came the frosty reply from just behind Liam, "it would give us both pleasure."

Startled, he turned to observe his sister standing just outside the door. He noticed her very becoming costume—a jonquil carriage dress, over which she wore a matching spencer—and not for the first time he was stunned to discover how grown-up she looked. Fast upon the heels of that thought came an even more surprising discovery—his usually adoring sister was angry with him. Her chin was at a belligerent angle and her pretty blue eyes held a decided look of censure.

"Miss Cordia," Champ said, rising to his feet and making her a bow. "How kind of you to accept my invitation."

"On the contrary," the damsel replied, brushing past her brother and crossing the room to offer the gentleman her hand. "It is you who are kind, sir. I have been longing this age for a breath of fresh air."

Champ bowed again. "I am at your disposal, ma'am."

Liam was rendered speechless by the sincere adoration he saw in his friend's eyes, and the obvious reciprocation of the sentiment on his sister's part. As if he needed further confirmation of the evidence before him, he turned to look at Emaline.

Understanding his confusion, Emaline smiled, then nodded her head.

"Enjoy your ride," she said, as though paving the way for their departure. "When you return, Cordia, perhaps Champ will be ready for that tea he refused to share with me."

"Of course," the young lady replied, brushing past her brother without so much as a word, and ushering her swain from the room with what Mrs. Pruett would surely have called unseemly haste.

Still bemused, Liam stared at the closed door. "Champ is calling upon my sister?"

"Yes," Emaline replied quietly.

"Are you telling me that all this time he was never interested in y— in any other lady?"

"I do not believe so. From their first meeting, he and Cordia were enchanted with one another. Or so it appeared to me." She raised her eyebrows, as if in question. "You do not approve?"

"Oh, no. Nothing of the sort. Champ's a wonderful fellow. Been my best friend since our Eton days."

Emaline breathed a sigh of relief. "I am glad you have no objections, for you must know that Cordia is a young woman who knows her own mind."

"Yes," he replied. Then, almost as if a weight had been lifted from his shoulders, Liam threw back his head and laughed. "Champ and Cordia. Who would have thought it?"

"Obviously, you did not," she said, smiling at the sound of his laughter.

Liam shook his head. "I had other things on my mind."

At the unexpected huskiness in his voice, a flush of warmth tiptoed up Emaline's spine. "You did?"

"Un-huh," he replied quietly.

She watched him come toward her, and the rhythm of

her heart quickened with excitement. When he paused only inches from her chair, she felt her entire body shudder with longing.

How much she had missed him! She wished she dared tell him how many times she had closed her eyes, trying to recapture the sound of his voice when he had called her his sweet love. She ached to hear the words again, if only to prove to herself that they were not some figment of her imagination—an imagination born of her love for him.

But he did not speak. When the silence stretched between them until she feared she might embarrass herself by begging him to tell her if he loved her, he reached out his hand to her. "Come," he said softly.

As if in a trance, Emaline put her hand in his and allowed him to pull her to her feet. For what seemed an eternity, they gazed into one another's eyes. Warm brown lost in the blue of the sky. Daylight and evening becoming one.

When she thought she would weep for the sheer joy of standing thus, he let go her hand and cradled her face in his palms, much as he had done two days ago. His touch was zephyr soft, a mere whisper of contact, yet it awakened every nerve in her body.

Gently his thumbs feathered across her brows, the mesmerizing strokes exhorting her eyelids to close, heightening her awareness. She breathed deeply, savoring the clean, fresh-air fragrance that clung to him, and while his very essence filled her senses, his thumbs smoothed their way across her cheeks to ply their magic upon her lips.

Emaline gasped as delicious shivers engulfed her. Sweet, sweet agony.

She felt his face draw near, so close his breath seemed to sear her flesh. Slowly, softly, he brushed his lips across hers, the tantalizing movement making her lightheaded.

Then, like a man denied too long, his arms stole around her, gathering her to him, molding her pliant body to the hardness of his, while his mouth captured hers.

Lost in a weightless, timeless world of joy, Emaline clung to him, her mind—her very soul—responding to his every touch.

They gave themselves up to this pleasurable pursuit for some little time, Emaline a willing pupil, Liam an impassioned instructor. When he finally forced himself to relinquish her lips, pressing his own against her temple, his breathing was labored. "My love," he whispered.

In no doubt, this time, as to the efficacy of her hearing, Emaline wound her arms around Liam's waist, laying her head upon his chest. Happy beyond her wildest dreams, she gave voice to the feelings of her heart.

"I love you," she said. "I think I began to love you almost from the first instant I saw you. And though I know you might look as high as you like for a wife, I want you to know that no one could ever love you as much as I do."

Liam's blood hummed with the sweet music of her words. He must be the luckiest man in the world, he decided, for he had just been given the most precious of gifts, at a time when he had the good sense to know its worth. Placing his fingers beneath her chin, he lifted her face so that he could feast his eyes upon her loveliness. "I could look no higher than you," he whispered.

Though his words warmed her heart, Emaline knew they were not true. "I am seven and twenty," she said. "Not a girl by anyone's standards."

"I know, love. And yet," he said, planting a kiss upon the tip of her pert nose, "lately I find very young ladies no longer catch my eye. Call it something lacking in my makeup, if you wish, but there it is. Give me a lady of seven and twenty any day. Or even eight and twenty!"

She looked up at him, as though to assure herself that he was taking the matter seriously. "And you might as well know this about me," she said, "I . . . I am a bit managing."

"No? You don't say so." He tried to still the movement of his ribs, for with her arms around him, she would know he was laughing.

"It is true. And there is one other thing I must tell you." Her face was pink with embarrassment. "It is a sort of confession."

"You may tell me anything," he said, giving no credence to the possibility that this innocent creature had ever done anything that required a confession.

"I tried to trick you," she said.

"Excuse me?"

"Actually, I tried to attract, captivate, and fascinate you. Only I was not very good at it. Mostly because I forgot to follow the book's instructions."

"Instructions? From a book?" He chuckled. "And here I was thinking our love was the work of fate. Truth to tell, I was on the very brink of adopting your theory of heavenly intervention."

She blushed again, and Liam was unable to resist the temptation to take her in his arms and kiss her until she was breathless. So dedicated was he to this intoxicating task that he nearly forgot they were standing in the middle of a drawing room where anyone might enter.

Putting her away from him, he found his own breathing not as steady as he could wish and decided to avail himself of the gold chair she had recently vacated. He solved the dilemma of where she should sit by gently guiding her onto his lap. She came willingly, and when he slipped his arms around her small waist, she was so obliging as to snuggle against him and rest her head against his shoulder.

"I assure you," he said, "that you have captivated me more with each passing day. As well, everything about you fascinates me. However, I find myself positively agog to discover the nature of this book you mentioned."

When she told him about finding the little book in the vitrine at Seymour Park, and about the times she had tried to practice the tactics espoused by Madame X, he was hard pressed not to laugh. "And there are ten chapters, you say?"

She nodded. "But I only got as far as Chapter Three. After that, I decided to send the book back to Wiltshire."

They were interrupted by a soft scratching at the door. "Yes?" Liam called, not granting the interloper permission to enter.

"Major?" Felix Harvey called through the door. "A package 'as arrived for you. From Rundall and Bridges. A very small package it is, but I thought as 'ow you might be desirous of 'aving it right away."

Without waiting for an answer, the valet opened the door a few inches, barely enough to allow his arm to slip through, then sent the small leather jeweler's box sailing across the room. To Emaline's surprise, Liam caught it in the air just above his head.

"It is for you," he said, opening the lid with one hand and holding it where she could see the contents. It was a ring. An exquisite sapphire surrounded by clear white diamonds.

Emaline held her breath, looking from the brilliant blue stone to her beloved's even more compelling eyes. "Liam, I—"

"You will marry me?" he said quickly. "That is what you were about to say? Right?"

"No," she said. Then seeing the pain in his eyes, she hurried to correct her statement. "What I mean is, yes, I will marry you. But that was not what I was about to say."

Relieved, Liam took the ring from its velvet bed and slipped it onto Emaline's finger, following the action with a kiss of such sweetness that at its conclusion he was led to ask her if she would agree to being married by special license.

"Yes," she answered breathlessly. "I will marry you any time and any place. But why? Is there a need to rush?"

"It is not the wedding I would hurry, my love, it is the wedding trip."

"Oh," she said, blushing rosily. Then, with an impish grin that delighted Liam beyond all reason, she said, "It was the wedding trip I wish to discuss. Or more to the point, it was Madame X's little book I wished to discuss."

"Yes, my love?"

"Liam, I have decided not to send the book back to Wiltshire."

"And why is that, my sweet?"

The imp was back in her eyes. "I wish to take it on our wedding trip."

"No need," he said, nibbling at an enticing spot just below her ear, "I could not possibly be more captivated than I am at this moment."

"I am delighted to hear it," she said. "However, there is something in Chapter Ten I especially wished to try . . . on my husband."

Liam threw back his head and laughed, joy filling his heart. "In that case, my love, I should not think of journeying so much as a mile without Chapter Ten."

Enchanted to discover that her husband-to-be had such an agreeable nature, Emaline decided to reward him for his forbearance by slipping her arms around his neck and surrendering her lips once again to his.